The Cooking Club Detectives

Ewa Jozefkowicz

ZEPHYR

An imprint of Head of Zeus

First published in the UK by Zephyr,
an imprint of Head of Zeus, in 2021

Text copyright © Ewa Jozefkowicz, 2021

9 7 5 3 1 2 4 6 8

A catalogue record for this book is available
from the British Library.

ISBN (PB): 9781789543605
ISBN (E): 9781789543599

Typeset by Ed Pickford
Cover artwork © Katy Riddell

Printed and bound in Great Britain
by CPI Group (UK) Ltd, Croydon CR0 4YY

Head of Zeus Ltd
5–8 Hardwick Street
London EC1R 4RG
WWW.HEADOFZEUS.COM

For the amazing staff at Magic Breakfast

One

When I first saw it, I thought it was the home of an artist, or maybe a fortune teller. I always imagined that they might live in peculiar ramshackle houses with colourful, patchwork curtains, ivy crawling up the walls and cats roaming around on the roof. And this is exactly the view that greeted me when I peered through the gap in the hedge that Tuesday morning. It was such an unexpected and beautiful sight that it made me gasp. I glimpsed a blue sign, not quite covered by the ivy that said, 'Skipton House Community Centre'.

A cold wind bit the air and I was exploring Milwood, our new village, for the first time. Later, I would remember it as the day when everything started to go wrong, but at that early hour, I didn't suspect a thing. I remember looking at my watch and seeing that it had just gone seven a.m. I couldn't believe that it was still so early as I'd been up for hours. I think on some level my brain was struggling to deal with all the newness. We'd only moved into the flat a week ago, and now I was starting secondary school. The estate still freaked me out – there was *sound* everywhere. It was an awful lot of sound for a place that was surrounded by what was mostly a big field.

My mum, Lara, would've probably flipped out about me going out on my own, especially as it was still half dark and I was only dressed in my school skirt, a T-shirt and a hoodie (the first things I could find) but she would never know if I made sure I was back before she woke up.

The field was practically on my front doorstep. It stretched from Milwood Road and was bordered by a river on the right. At the far end was a line of small, squat terraced houses, that looked as if they came from another century, and on the left-hand side, was a main road – if you could call it that – Dunstan Row. I'd seen its overgrown sign and was intrigued. I decided to turn into it, hoping that it might lead somewhere interesting. And it did.

Skipton House was almost hidden by dense bushes, and I would have walked right past it if I hadn't heard laughter coming from behind the hedge. First there was a giggle and then I heard someone singing a song. Before I knew it, I was edging closer, trying to take a peep through the misted window with the patchwork curtains.

Upon closer inspection, I saw it had three floors and it seemed there were quite a few people in there. The voices were young – kids my age. Someone was playing the guitar, then there was a clatter of plates, a clap of hands and an older voice talking over the noise.

I hadn't even realised I'd got so close. I was about three steps away from the window when something furry brushed against my leg and my heart lurched. I looked down to see one of the two cats I'd spotted earlier on the roof weaving a figure of eight around my legs. I must have yelped, because suddenly the misted window was flung open and a boy's puzzled face appeared. He had olive skin, a shock of black curly hair and deep brown eyes, which looked at me questioningly.

'Want to come in?' he asked simply.

I frantically shook my head. And before I could think about what I was doing, my feet were already stepping away, pounding the grass at an increasing pace. I burst through the gap in the hedge and ran all the way down the road to our estate. I didn't stop until I'd pelted up the three flights of stairs to our new flat and banged the door behind me. I slid down the back of it and gulped mouthfuls of air.

But what had I been so scared of? The boy hadn't seemed cross and he'd invited me in. I'd acted like a complete chicken, running off like that. He must have thought I was mad. I only hoped he wasn't in my year at school. I could do without having to deal with any additional awkwardness.

It had been Lara's idea to move here. She'd been promoted at Rodrigo's and she'd always said that the first thing we'd do when she'd earned a bit of extra money, was to move to a bigger place, where I could have my own bedroom and everything. It sounded amazing, but the only two-bed place we could afford was miles away not just from school and my friends, but also any form of proper civilization. Lara's commute into work now took over an hour, but she said that it was worth it. She'd admitted to me that sales at Rodrigo's had been down, and that he'd given her the promotion in the hope that she might turn the shop around. I couldn't help but think that it was risky. What if she couldn't save it from shutting down?

'I think I can boost the sales,' she said to me. 'It's about getting the right clothes in and offering a few promotional discounts. Plus, you and I need a new start, eh?' she asked, looking genuinely excited, and that was that. I didn't dare say anything to put her off.

That morning when I first saw Skipton House, Lara was in her usual deep sleep. She didn't even wake up when I slammed the door behind me after my morning escapade. In fact, she only emerged from her bedroom when I was putting on my shoes and I was surprised to see her up that early. Tuesdays were her only proper lie-in days, as the Deputy Manager opened the shop.

'Hey, hey – what's happening?' Her sleepy, unmade-up face appeared in the living room doorway.

'Nothing. Getting ready to go into school. How come you're up?'

'I set my alarm so that I could whip you up some breakfast. It's a big day for you! D'you want eggs?'

'You didn't have to,' I muttered, and then when she looked disappointed, I added, 'I'm so nervous, I couldn't eat a thing.'

'I don't like you going without breakfast. Here, take this,' she said, putting some dried apples and almonds into a snack box and handing them to me. 'Hey, it's going to be an adventure! You'll meet great new people and you'll make loads of friends.'

'I hope so.'

'Those kids would be mad not to jump at the chance to be mates with you.'

And then she enveloped me in a hug. She still smelled like the lime from the pie that she'd made yesterday and, as she ruffled my hair, I felt that things would work out. There were moments, just like that one, when she was the same as every other mum. Only I knew that she was anything but.

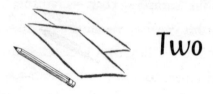

Two

'You have a cool surname. Where did that come from?' the girl sitting next to me in geography asked.

'Oh, erm thanks – it's Italian,' I told her, feeling the heat rise in my face. I prayed she wouldn't ask anything else about it, but the question I was dreading soon came.

'Does it mean anything? The word sounds kind of familiar.'

'Well, yeah. Bellissima means "beautiful".'

Ever since Lara had told me this years ago, it had made me cringe inside. Anyone would think I should be pleased, right? Wrong. I was really self-conscious about it because I'd always been gangly looking, with long arms and legs, and elbows sticking out at awkward angles. Throughout primary school, I was a head taller than most of the kids in our class, and that included the boys. I suppose Lara is tall too, so maybe I get it from her, but she always seems to move gracefully like the beautiful gazelles you see on nature programmes, not like me – the human daddy longlegs.

But Tanya, my new desk companion, clearly didn't guess my thoughts. 'It's awesome,' she said. She had gorgeous earth brown skin, and long plaits arranged in two neat buns. I noticed how brand new her school uniform was, the shirt collar neatly ironed, the skirt expertly taken up so it was just the right length to be within the school rules, but not long enough to be uncool. Lara had taken great care washing and ironing my second-hand uniform, but even without looking at my reflection in the window, I could tell how scruffy I was in comparison.

'Thanks,' I muttered.

I'd begged Lara not to send me here. I'd wanted to go to Mayhurst, like most of the other kids from my primary school, but she'd insisted on Fieldway, because it was closest to our new flat – Mayhurst would have been a forty-five minute drive each way.

I didn't normally get nervous, but when I went through the school gates for the first time, I could already feel my heart in my stomach. I knew how important it would be to make a good first impression – it might be my only chance of making friends. At primary school I'd never had a best friend, but at least I'd had a group I'd always hung around with and I knew everyone. Here, I felt like I was lost at sea.

'Are you OK?' asked Tanya, when we were spilling out of the classroom for break. 'You look pale.'

'Oh, yeah, fine,' I said, too quickly and she raised an eyebrow.

'I'm going to check out the vending machines,' she said. 'Want to come?'

I nodded and followed her along the corridor to the hallway of the canteen, when another girl – small and black-haired – gave a squeal of delight and launched herself at Tanya.

'Ohmigod ohmigod. I've been looking for you

everywhere. I'm so gutted that we're not in the same class. You know, I even got Mum to write to Mr Kelly to ask if I could be moved, but he said that our allocated classes were final. So we only get to see each other at break and lunch. Anyway, you need to fill me in on totally like everything. I'm dying to hear what Jamaica was like. Were you there with Tom's family? *Please* tell me about the older brother.'

Tanya hugged her back, but she didn't respond to her greeting in the same hysterical way.

'I will. I will. It's good to see you, Ali. Hey, this is Erin. She doesn't really know anyone here yet.'

Ali gave me a disinterested look. She linked arms with Tanya and fished around in her pocket with her other hand. It suddenly hit me that I'd obviously need money for the vending machines. I didn't have any.

I must have looked panicked because Tanya asked, 'Did you forget your cash? Don't worry, I can let you borrow some. Dad's given me a tenner.'

It was only when I looked at the rows of neatly arranged chocolate bars in the machine, that I realised I hadn't eaten anything since supper the night before. Hunger was probably one of the main reasons for me feeling so sick. I searched around in my bag for the snack box that Lara had given me, but I couldn't find it. I must have left it on the kitchen table.

'Thanks. I'll make sure I pay you back tomorrow.'

'No worries.'

In the end, she bought us both an apple and a packet of crisps and we sat down together at her desk in the form room. Ali kept nattering on about travelling around Iceland with her parents and some family friends, but her memories seemed to mainly feature her dad's friend's son, who was fifteen and had gone on the trip with them.

'He sat next to me in the back for the whole thing,' she said, glancing over at Tanya to check whether she looked impressed. I was surprised to see that she didn't. 'I'll show you a photo later. Anyway, what about Jamaica?'

'Oh, it was great – boiling hot and the tastiest food! The jerk chicken was insanely good. And before you ask, Tom and his brother were acting really stupid – most of the time they were dive-bombing in the pool and being told off by the hotel manager.'

I could tell that Ali was disappointed with this answer and wanted to ask more questions about Tom, but Tanya cut her off.

'Hey Erin, what did you do over the summer?'

I secretly wished that she hadn't asked. I hadn't gone anywhere like Iceland or Jamaica. I'd spent most of the six weeks either helping in the stockroom at Rodrigo's, reading or hanging out on the playground of our old estate. I did go to Harrogate for a long weekend with Lara to visit one of her old school friends who'd recently had a baby.

'Not much really. We went up to Yorkshire for a few days. Then we were moving house, so it got a bit chaotic.'

'Oh really? Where did you move from?'

'North London.' I figured the less detail I gave, the better.

'Oh, from the Big Smoke?' said Ali. 'It must be really boring for you round here in our little town. And where do you live now?'

'On the Milwood Estate,' I said, hoping that she didn't know where it was.

'Behind the big playing fields, next to the river?' she asked, wrinkling her nose. 'I've heard it's dodgy round there. Do you live in one of the Alms Houses?'

'Alms Houses? No, what are those?'

'They're a row of old houses at the bottom of the field near the community centre. I've heard they're dirty with mould climbing the walls and that tramps live in them, but it's probably not true,' said Ali, looking meaningfully in Tanya's direction.

'Of course it's not true,' said Tanya, ignoring her. 'That area's really nice. There are some great views from the top of the hill. I'm jealous that you're so close to it. I love that place.'

It didn't make me feel much better. I had a suspicion that there would always be an invisible barrier between Tanya and Ali's world, and mine.

Three

Lara wasn't home when I got back. I opened the fridge, hoping to find some leftovers of her lasagne, but there were only tomatoes and mozzarella that she must have been saving for one of her tray bakes, a couple of yoghurts and some ham.

She clearly hadn't done the shopping which she'd promised to do the day before, which meant that our system was messed up. Lara usually did a big food shop on Sunday and we had a rotation of quick weekday meals which went like this:

Monday – veggie pizza with red onions, tomatoes, cheddar cheese and sometimes aubergine. I like it spicy so I add chili flakes!

Tuesday – chicken kievs and sweet potato chips with salad. Sweet potato chips are even more tasty than regular ones. If I'm feeling adventurous, I might even make carrot chips.

Wednesday – macaroni and cheese. I like experimenting with unusual cheeses. Blue cheeses are the weirdest but also the best.

Thursday – Welsh stew based on Grandma's recipe. It always reminds me a little of her, even though I barely remember her.

Friday – chicken or veggie curry, made with Lara's special sauce which is a spicier take on korma.

Lara insists that everything has to be home-made. She likes knowing exactly what ingredients go into every meal, and she feels that cooking makes the whole process of eating so much nicer, which I agree with. So these recipes formed our typical week, but Lara always loves adding her special touches.

Lara worked every Saturday until seven p.m, but she had almost every Sunday off (unless Mr Rodrigo himself was on holiday and she had to cover). On Saturdays, I used to spend full days at a friend's house and when Lara collected me after work, she was knackered, so we would treat ourselves to a takeaway. When we lived in our old flat, we had our favourite restaurant, Thaisty, which we'd been going to for years. They always knew our favourites – chicken pad Thai for me and prawn green curry for Lara. I was on a mission to find us an equivalent here. Sunday we made fish and chips.

On weekdays (apart from Mondays), Lara always opened the shop so she had to be up early. But the good news was that she finished work at four, so she was home only slightly later than me and we could start cooking. I always looked forward to this part of the day most. We would catch up on everything that had happened – I would tell her about school and she'd tell me about some of the funny customers that had been in the shop that day, like the lady who always brought her four dogs with her. Lara said that she reminded her a little of Grandma.

My memories of her are tiny fragments, little slivers of fish trying to dart away, but there are some things I'll always remember – a warm lap, a waft of rose perfume, the soft curl of long, blonde hair. Grandma was never properly grey – she didn't get a chance to be. She was only fifty-five when she died, which is extremely young. She had an aneurysm which is a complicated word for a bulge in a blood vessel in your brain. Lara says that the only blessing is that it happened so fast that Grandma wouldn't have suffered. She still cries when she talks about her and then she gets cross at herself because she has to redo her make-up.

Anyhow, Grandma died when I was four and since then, we've managed pretty well. The only thing that bothered Lara was how cramped our old flat was. I also knew how much she loved cooking and I could tell she wished she had time to properly devote to trying out new dishes. And, yeah, well I guess I am the reason for her not being able to.

The flat situation was solved about six months ago, when she got promoted to a manager role at Rodrigo's. We could afford to move into a bigger place, and even get some new furniture and a widescreen TV. Unlike our old flat, which was a humongous mess, this one was sparkling clean. Without even talking about it, it seemed that we both decided at the same time that we would take special care of it. I vacuum once a week and do the dusting, and Lara cleans the kitchen and does the tidying and washing. That's why I was surprised to see that she'd left the living room in a state when I came home after my first day at school. Her cup and plate were lying on the coffee table, her pyjamas were strewn over the sofa, and she'd left some magazines and her notebook on the floor, with pages spilling out at random. I picked one up. It was a recipe for lamb pie. I tidied everything up and put a bunch of wildflowers that I'd collected from the field next to our house in one of her favourite little glass vases. But still there was no sign of her.

I thought of going out to get the remaining ingredients for the chicken kievs, but then I wondered if she was already planning to get them herself on the way home. In the end, I made myself a cheese toastie and went to my room to start my geography homework. I couldn't believe that we'd been set something on the first day. But I was less cross when I realised that it was actually interesting. We were supposed to write down our thoughts on what made a good map, and to come up with our own idea for a unique map which we'd work on in tomorrow's lesson.

I whipped out Grandma's old atlas and took another look at the double-page spread of the entire globe. It had the capital cities marked on it and the highest mountains. I'd always loved comparing the sizes of different countries. It's extraordinary to see how big Greenland is, and that the whole of Australia is pretty much the same size as central Europe.

I flipped over to the first country page, which is Afghanistan (because the countries are listed in alphabetical order), and saw a photo of its national dish – pulao, which is steamed rice with raisins and carrots, usually served with a side dish of meat, vegetables or beans. I knew straight away what my map would be – a wonderful visual display of foods eaten in different countries, from Spanish paella to Japanese sushi. One day, Lara and I would travel to these places and sample every dish, bringing the best elements back to our restaurant. I did a first sketch of it and still Lara wasn't back.

By then, I began to sense that something was up so I tried her phone. It rang through, and I left a message. I tried her a couple more times in the next hour, beginning to feel panicked. Awful scenes ran through my mind of Lara in hospital after a car accident, or being held hostage by some scary gang. Maybe one of the dodgy people from the Alms Houses had got her as she walked home from work!

I thought about whether to ring Aunty Sarah to tell her what had happened. Although she was on the other side of the world these days, she would definitely know how to help. As I was checking what the time was in Sydney, a message from Lara came through.

Sorry. Sorry. On my way home.

It was 10.15 p.m. when the key finally turned in the lock. Lara came into my room when she saw that my bedside light was on. I could tell straight away from the look on her face that something terrible had happened.

'I'm sorry, Erin. I've had a really awful day. I totally lost track of the time, because I had some bad news, but that's no excuse. I should have messaged you sooner. Anyway, how was your first day?' she asked nervously, sitting on the edge of my bed and pulling off her heeled boots.

'Erm, OK ish,' I said. I already had my mouth open ready to tell her about Tanya and Ali, and how I didn't fit in, but then I looked at her smudged eyes and I could tell she'd been crying.

'What happened?' I asked her.

'Rodrigo let me go.'

'What, why?' I sat bolt upright. I'd been dreading this situation ever since Lara had told me that the shop was doing badly.

'I suppose I should have seen it coming. I could tell that we had fewer and fewer customers but I stupidly held out hope that the promotions I'd been coming up with might work. Anyway, the sales decline means Rodrigo has to cut the staff right down.'

'But... but you've worked there for years.'

'Exactly. I'm the most expensive member of staff. That's why. I talked to Rodrigo for ages trying to persuade him to let me stay. I said that I would reduce my hours, or even take a pay cut, but he said that he'd already thought about all of the options and that it wouldn't be enough. I think he felt guilty about having promoted me, when he had a strong suspicion that this would happen. About six months ago, I kept telling him how much we needed a bigger place, and I wonder if that drove his decision about the promotion. I shouldn't have been so reckless. Anyway,' she sighed, 'maybe it's a sign. I'll be thirty-five next year, Erin. Maybe it's high time I gave cooking a proper shot.'

It was too much information at once. My head was swimming with the new facts and I was desperately trying to figure out what new changes this situation would bring to our lives, which had already changed so much recently.

'What does this mean?' I dared to ask. 'Will you apply for a role in a restaurant?' We lived in the wrong place for that kind of thing. There were only a few pubs, a café and a couple of restaurants which looked like they were family-run. They would be unlikely to take Lara on.

'I have some savings. I also have loads of recipe ideas and I thought I might enter the Cookathon. Is that mad? I thought that if I don't try, I won't know if I'm actually any good. It's what I've always wanted to do, Erin. But…'

'But what?'

She paused, as if unsure how to continue.

'Things always stood in the way, I suppose,' she said eventually. 'We needed money and I couldn't guarantee enough of it through starting at the very bottom in a restaurant kitchen. Plus the hours would have been completely wrong. And entering a competition would have been risky. Anyway, if it doesn't work out, I can always get another silly retail job, can't I?'

I couldn't believe she was actually considering the Cookathon. We watched it every Friday night and Lara was always commenting on what changes she would make to each contestant's dish. But I'd never actually imagined that she would consider taking part herself.

'It wasn't a silly retail job. It was "high fashion", you said it yourself. You were always so good at it, and Rodrigo loves you.'

'I know, but it's not what I imagined doing long term,' she said honestly.

'Well, if you want to do the Cookathon, you should go for it,' I said, although my voice came out shaky and the flutter in my stomach was getting worse.

'No matter what happens, we'll be fine,' said Lara, hugging me tightly. 'We always are.'

I knew she meant well, but those last words of hers made me feel even more nervous, because I could hear in the tone of her voice, that she wasn't sure at all.

And to top it off, a gnawing feeling of guilt stayed with me after Lara had left the room. I'd always known that she loved cooking – this love filled our daily lives and resulted in hundreds of delicious dishes – but I'd never realised how much she'd wanted to do it as a career. And it dawned on me what she meant by 'things' always standing in her way. It wasn't so much 'things' but people, or more specifically, one person. Me.

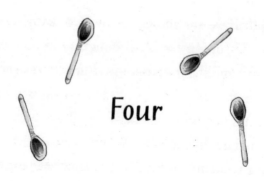

Four

Next morning, I was woken by Lara gently shaking my shoulder and calling my name. I'd been in the depths of a disturbing dream in which I was standing in a vast field outside an overgrown building. Through its misted window, I could make out the familiar silhouette of a woman, dark against the bright lights. I felt my stomach rumbling with hunger and I drew closer in the hope that she might offer me something to eat. The closer I got, the more I could see – blonde hair, an apron, a table filled with bowls, wooden spoons, fresh vegetables and pots of various ingredients. Before I knew it, my face was pressed to the window, peering straight into the room, and I realised with surprise that the woman was Lara. The radio was playing

and she sang as she cooked. And then I caught sight of trophies lining the wall. One was in the shape of a knife and fork crossed together and another was a chef's hat. There were also rows of framed certificates hanging on the wall.

I knocked on the glass. At first she didn't hear me, so I tried again, louder this time. Finally, she spotted me and smiled, but her smile was different to the one I knew so well. It was only when she opened the window and said, 'Lovely to meet you. Would you like to come in and try some of my food?' that a cold chill ran through me. This famous and successful version of Lara didn't know me.

'You'll be late, Erin. Come on, up up up!'

'What? What's the time?'

'Almost eight.'

I picked up my phone from the bedside table and saw that the battery had died. I must have forgotten to charge it. It was very unlike me to sleep in. And then the memory of everything that had happened yesterday began to flood in.

'How come you're up?' I muttered.

'I couldn't sleep. I was up at five a.m. working on my application for the Cookathon. I reckon if I want to give it a shot, I need to hit the ground running.'

'Right.'

'But I also had time to make you egglets. Get dressed quickly and you can have them in the kitchen. Wrap yourself some up for lunch too.'

Egglets was the name that we'd given to Lara's small round omelettes made with ham, eggs and a sprinkling of chives. They were little circles of amazement. When I was tiny I used to pretend they were UFOs, travelling to the moon but getting sucked into the black hole of my mouth on the way. Today, they made me forget, if only for a few minutes, about the two worries that had been circling each other in my mind. The first was to do with our money running out because of Lara not having a job, and the second was to do with the Cookathon, which I remembered as being horribly cut-throat.

Eggsquisite Egglets

Ingredients

- 3 eggs
- 1 teaspoon sunflower oil
- 1 teaspoon butter
- 1 pack of sliced ham
- 50g cheddar cheese, grated
- A handful of chives (for sprinkling)

Method

1. Beat the eggs well in a bowl and add a pinch of salt and pepper.

2. Heat the butter and oil in a non-stick frying pan on medium heat — wait until the butter has melted and is foaming.

3. Pour the eggs into the pan, tilt it a little from side to side to allow the eggs to swirl and cover the surface of the pan completely. Let it cook for about twenty seconds and then draw a line down the middle with the edge

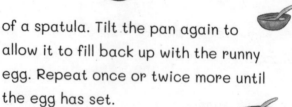

of a spatula. Tilt the pan again to allow it to fill back up with the runny egg. Repeat once or twice more until the egg has set.

4. Now sprinkle on grated cheese and pieces of chopped up ham and chopped chives. If you want to, add a dollop of ketchup. Then, fold the whole thing in half with a spatula.

5. Here's the best bit: remove it from the pan onto a plate, and use a small, sharp circular cutter to cut the big omelette into little egglets. You can have loads of fun eating the discarded edges.

Through the first two periods of English, my mind kept conjuring up Lara on TV, making one of her mouth-watering chicken pies and then winning and being given a job in some fancy restaurant in London. But what would happen then? Would we have to move again?

After break we had geography and Tanya had saved me a seat again.

'Right, maps,' said Mr Chandler from the front of the class. He was a young man, I guessed around Lara's age, with neat, dark hair and an impressive beard. He laughed in a way that made me instantly like him. I was glad that I had him not only as our geography teacher, but also as form tutor.

'I hope you find them as interesting as I do,' he continued. 'Of course today, you have access to so many weird and wonderful maps online. If you go on Google Earth, you can see your own house on the screen. You can even look at the surface of Mars on an interactive map and there are phone apps that map the paths of rockets being launched into space.

'But think back to what maps were like fifty, one hundred, a thousand years ago. They relied on a whole range of different people going around and measuring distances – then trying to plot those distances on paper. It seemed incredibly hard and there was a big margin for error. Anyway, we're going to spend the first lesson working on your ideas for special, interesting maps and I'll be looking for volunteers to present theirs at the end of the lesson.'

Tanya drew a copy of the London Tube map and started filling in the names of famous people who had lived near each station. It was a great idea, but I saw that she was struggling to find people for a few of them. I didn't even recognise some of the names she'd put down.

Alice, who sat two rows in front of me, volunteered to be the first one to present her work – she talked us through her map of the world which showed the most and least densely populated areas. China and India glowed bright red, while Iceland was the palest blue.

A tall boy called Ben presented his map showing the locations of ancient historical kingdoms, and Shona showed us her scary, futuristic map of what the world would look like if climate change continued at the current rate.

And then a boy with a shock of dark curly hair stood up and presented my idea exactly. He wasn't from our form as we had mixed sets for geography, but he looked oddly familiar. He passed around his beautifully illustrated map of the national dishes in different countries, highlighting the way in which climate and crops affected food. It was far more detailed and well thought through than mine. I really hoped Mr Chandler wouldn't choose me to present. The boy was talking about why he'd decided to focus on food when suddenly, he looked straight at me and I froze.

He was the boy I'd seen in the window of the crumbling house. He gave me a puzzled look, as if he was trying to work out where he knew me from. I looked down at my desk, not meeting his eyes.

'Thank you, Frixos. You've reminded me about a notice I was going to give at form time, but I may as well tell you now while we're on the subject. If anyone is interested, we have Cooking Club running after school every Thursday in the community centre. It's a ten-minute walk from school and it's run by Mrs Gupta, who is one of our school chefs. It was pretty popular last year, so we've decided to keep it going. It's free, it lasts an hour, and of course you get to eat the food you've made. If you're interested, put your name down on the notice board in your form room, so that we can get an idea of numbers.'

'Awesome,' said Frixos, giving Mr Chandler a double thumbs up, 'I'll be there.'

I wanted to put my name down too. The club was perfect for two obvious reasons – I loved cooking, and it would give me the opportunity to meet people in a different setting. It was also a chance to check if Frixos had recognised me, and if so, to explain myself. I couldn't avoid him for ever.

I ended up sitting next to Ali and Tanya again at lunch, and they watched me as I whipped Lara's egglets out of my bag.

'What are those?' Ali asked, pretending to be disgusted.

'They're mini omelettes. My mum made them this morning. These ones have ham inside and a little bit of broccoli. You can add mozzarella too, or peppers... or whatever you want really. They're obviously not as good as when they've first been made, but they're still delicious. Do you want to try one?'

'Er, no thanks,' said Ali.

I could tell that Tanya looked tempted, but she shook her head, so I took a big bite myself.

'What's your favourite food then?' I asked when I'd wolfed the first one.

'Oh I don't know. There are so many,' said Ali rolling her eyes. 'I'd probably have to start by deciding the cuisine, so that would be... Thai. No, actually Italian, because I love pasta. I could eat it with any kind of sauce, although I think my favourite is pappardelle with meatballs. They did a delicious version of it when we went to Tuscany last year. It was totally delicious. We would eat it while we watched the sun set, out in our garden next to the pool.'

'Do you make it at home, with your parents?' I was genuinely curious.

'Oh, my mum tries to cook, but she can't make Italian. It always ends up tasting weird.'

'If you like it, you could try to do it yourself,' I suggested seriously, but Ali narrowed her eyes, and looked at me as if to check whether I was making fun of her.

'And you?' I asked Tanya. 'What do you like cooking at home?'

'Ana usually makes dinner, unless it's a weekend and then we have takeaway. My favourite is prawn korma – we have a really good Indian down the road. Super tasty and you can tell that it's made from really good, fresh ingredients.'

'Who's Ana?' I asked, and then wondered whether I shouldn't have been so nosey. But Tanya didn't seem to mind.

'She's our housekeeper and she was also mine and my brother's nanny when we were younger. Our mum died when I was six and Jayden was three.'

She said it quite matter-of-factly, but I was still stunned.

'Oh my goodness. I'm sorry,' I said. I reached to hold her hand across the table and she didn't stop me.

'Thanks. It was a long time ago now. Anyway, how come you're asking about favourite dishes?'

'Well, I love cooking. I actually thought that I might join the cooking club,' I admitted and then immediately regretted it when I saw the look on their faces.

'What? Are you serious? You know it's at the community centre?' said Ali, repulsed.

'So? I thought I might learn how to make some stuff that I haven't eaten before.'

'Well, I'm definitely not going to bother with that. I have loads of better things that I can think of doing with my time,' she said, picking at her salad.

'I'll come with you,' said Tanya unexpectedly, in the middle of eating her yoghurt. 'You never know. It might be interesting.'

'Awesome.' I felt, for the first time since we'd moved, something positive was happening.

'Where's the community centre anyway?'

'It's actually near where you live. It's some old, converted house across the field from the Alms Houses. I've never actually been myself, but I've heard it looks really weird,' said Ali.

'Weird how?'

'Oh, you know, overgrown, cats wandering around everywhere.'

'Come on, it's not that bad. It's kind of quirky. I love their patchwork curtains. They were made by Mrs Barlow, who used to be a teacher at our school,' said Tanya. 'Besides, the place is really important to loads of people. They have free day care there, and music breakfasts for kids who might otherwise come to school hungry, and loads of sports clubs and dance societies too.'

That was when it clicked into place – I remembered the blue sign outside the front door and knew exactly where they were talking about. I was more curious than ever to find out what happened behind its doors.

Five

I could hear noises coming from our flat as I walked up the stairs and at first I freaked out that someone had broken in, but then I remembered that Lara was home and probably had been for most of the day.

As I opened the door, I was greeted by the radio on full blast, steam coming out of the kitchen, and Lara fiddling frantically with something on her phone. The image from my dream came back to me and I felt sick.

'Hiya, love,' she shouted, turning down the volume. When she came over to give me a hug, I saw that she'd styled her hair and done her 'night out' make-up. She looked incredible and I hoped that there was a chance that one day I might grow up to look even a little bit like her. Lara had once told me that she was awkward and gangly too at my age, but I wonder whether she was trying to make me feel better.

'Are you going out somewhere?' I asked her.

'What? Oh no, this is for the photo. I tried to do a selfie, but they look rubbish, so I thought I'd better wait for you to get home so that you can take a photo of me in action.'

'In action?'

'As in cooking. Look, I'm making my fajitas. Can you do a couple of snaps on my phone and then help me with the lighting and colour filters? You're so good at that stuff. I need them for my profile page for the Cookathon. It's so that the judges can easily recognise contestants from the pictures. I'll tell you about my application in a sec. You won't believe it, but one of the organisers actually called me this morning. I'd barely sent it when the phone went.'

'Really? Why so fast?'

'Here's the thing – they have auditions once a month usually, as they select the contestants for each mini-series, and then you wait at least a couple of months to hear back, but literally about an hour after they'd received my application, they rang me back to say that someone had dropped out and asked if I was available on *Friday*. Friday – d'you understand, Erin? That's in three days' time! I agreed on the spot because I was so dumbstruck, but now I'm thinking that I'm mad. I need time to prepare.'

I ended up taking about seven or eight different pictures of Lara in different poses. We had Lara holding a spoon, Lara peering carefully into a pan of sauce, Lara smiling as she sprinkled grated cheese on her fajita, and a whole range of others.

'You have a real skill, you know,' said Lara, admiring them. 'I usually hate people taking photos of me, but you capture the scene in a really natural way.'

'It's because I see things in a way that other people don't.'

It was true. I'd noticed over the years that I often spotted things that my friends missed and that my memory was particularly good. Even when I was little and I used to play 'spot the difference' with some of the kids at school, I would get the answers within a minute. Once in Year Six we did a test online where you filled out the answers to about thirty questions and it gave you some suggestions for jobs that you might like to do in the future. It was only meant to be a bit of fun, but for me the top answer was 'detective' – I guess I had some pretty strong detective qualities.

'Am I mad for saying "yes" to them?' asked Lara.

'No! You've been doing this for years. Look at all the recipes you've written,' I added, pointing to her notepad.

'Maybe it's a sign that things are going to work out.'

'Want me to come with you?'

'You know I'd love that, but it's Friday and you have school. Also, I'm so nervous that I probably need to be on my own. I can do my breathing exercises on the train there.'

'OK, that's fair enough. But I can come to the live shows?'

'That's assuming I get in! But yeah, of course. You can come to the live shows.'

And then we sat down to eat Lara's fajitas which were getting cold but were as delicious as always. She told me that it had taken her ages to decide which dish to pick for the audition.

'I thought about doing one of my pies, but then I realised the fajitas are more unusual. On the phone they said that they mainly contacted me because I "cooked on a budget" and they thought viewers would like that, so I wanted to show them the delicious things you can make with ingredients that don't cost very much. I think this is the sort of dish that shows that the most.'

'It totally does,' I agreed, finding the page in Lara's recipe book.

Lara's Fantabulous Fajitas

Ingredients

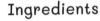

- 1 onion
- 1 red pepper
- 2 chicken breasts
- 1 tablespoon honey

- 1 sachet of Fajita spice mix
- 1 pack of wraps
- 50g cheddar cheese, grated

Method

1. Chop the onion into strips. If you've never done it before, ask someone for help and be super careful with the knife, always cutting away from your fingers. Then chop your pepper in half and take out the seeds. Cut it into strips.

2. Cut the chicken breasts into cubes. *Tip:* using kitchen scissors is quicker than using a knife and much safer too. If you don't eat meat, replace the chicken with tofu.

3. Heat a little oil in a frying pan and drop the onion in. Then add a big spoonful of honey and fry for a couple of minutes, until the onion is browned and nicely coated in honey.

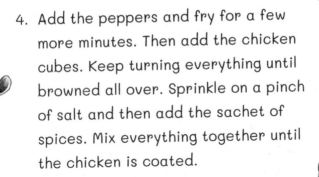

4. Add the peppers and fry for a few more minutes. Then add the chicken cubes. Keep turning everything until browned all over. Sprinkle on a pinch of salt and then add the sachet of spices. Mix everything together until the chicken is coated.

5. Turn off the heat and leave to cool for five minutes. Then grab a wrap, put a few spoonfuls of the chicken mix in the middle of it, add the grated cheese, roll it up and enjoy!

'This is the best batch that you've made,' I said. 'I think fajitas might have risen to my favourite recipe of yours.'

'No way! You're not just saying that?'

'Come on, you know that I don't just say things,' I said, nudging her in the ribs.

'Well then, it must be the right choice for the Cookathon, Erin!'

'There you go – always at your service. Hey, I'm joining Cooking Club,' I told her. 'It's run by one of the chefs at school. It's on Thursday nights in that weird building at the end of Dunstan Row – you know the overgrown one, covered in ivy? It's apparently a community centre.'

'Nice. I had a community centre where I grew up – they did lots of sports activities, but sadly no cooking club. I would have loved it if they did. But d'you know what I reckon?' she said. 'You could probably run that club.'

'Come on, I'm nowhere near that good.'

'You are. One day you'll be much better than me, if you're not already. But then again, you have learned from the master,' she added with a wink. 'Hey, you haven't told me what the kids at school are like. Have you made any new friends?'

'One so far – Tanya. At least it seems like she wants to be my friend, although it's weird, because we haven't really got anything in common. But I like talking to her. I feel there's more to her than you see at first glance. Have you ever had a friend like that?'

'Let me think… When I was about your age I was friends with a boy who lived in our block. I suppose we did have a little bit in common, in that he lived with his dad and I lived with my mum, and neither of us had a great deal of money – but our interests were completely different. He loved playing football, and being a troublemaker with his friends from school, and I was much more of a home girl, always trying to help my mum in the kitchen. But we met because we lived so close and we were kind of inseparable until he moved away. We would spend hours sitting on the wall outside our block chatting. Your grandma would always say that I was the one who helped him sort himself out and encouraged him to do something with his life, but I'm not sure that's fair. I maybe set him on the right path, but he did the rest himself.'

'What did you do?' I asked, intrigued.

'He was always playing football and even without knowing much about it, I could see that he was very good, head and shoulders above the others. I told him that he should do something with it. But he didn't believe in himself and kept coming up with excuses – the main one was that he had no money to sign up for proper coaching. So I found him a local club run by that community centre that I was telling you about, and told him that I'd bake him his favourite banana bread if he gave it a try. He said that he'd do it just for that. But anyway, he ended up loving the club and he was spotted there by a talent scout from the local team, so he ended up playing professionally.'

'That's awesome. That's why you always associate banana bread with celebrations. So what's he doing now? How come I've never met him?'

'I don't know. We lost touch, when he moved away. I haven't actually thought about him in ages, not until you asked me that question. But I guess that he played an important part in my life too, because he was the only person apart from my mum who told me that my cooking was pretty decent. And because he was always speaking his mind, I knew that he was telling the truth – it was a real compliment.'

'And now you're doing something with it,' I said, feeling guilty that Lara hadn't yet had her moment in the way that her friend had.

When we were washing up, I asked her about the

plan for Friday and the mood suddenly changed. Lara tried to keep her voice steady, but her hands were shaking with nerves.

'I need to get up early and head down to the studios in Chelsea. There will be forty cooks there, and we're supposed to turn up at nine a.m. for registration. Then at ten a.m, we select our ingredients from the market, and we each do a short presentation to the judges. Then the real "cooking" starts at eleven a.m. and we have exactly one and a half hours to make our starter and dessert, which is loads of time really.'

'What will you do for dessert? Your lucky banana bread?'

'Banana bread is only for super special occasions,' she said, seriously. 'I was thinking of making my "carrot cake with a twist", but I might change my mind when I see the ingredients on offer.'

'Won't the cake take too long?' I asked, and immediately regretted the question. I didn't want to make her more nervous than she already was.

'No, it should be fine. I just need to watch my timing.'

That night, I did something that I hadn't done in a really long time. I crossed my fingers and toes for Lara, because I could tell that she wanted to win this more than I could have ever imagined.

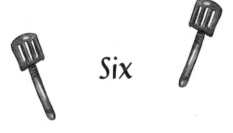

Six

On Thursday a group of us who were keen to join Cooking Club gathered by the school's main entrance.

There were more people than I'd expected – I counted about twenty, and I could see that even Mr Chandler was amazed at the turnout. I recognised a few kids from our year, including Frixos. He was chatting to a tall ginger-haired boy whose face was covered in dense freckles.

'Hey, the runaway girl,' he said grinning at me, and I felt like running away again. 'You should have come in and joined us that morning. Why did you leg it like that?'

'What did you do?' asked Tanya, meeting my eye. We walked directly behind the boys, who kept turning around to chat to us.

'I was walking by Skipton the other morning, before I even knew what the building was. I heard voices, and I went closer to see...'

'... And then I invited her in through the window, but she got scared and ran away!'

'Maybe she didn't want to come in through the window,' said Tanya.

'No – I opened the window to invite her. She could have come in through the door,' he said, laughing. 'Anyway, I'm Frixos. And this is Sam.'

Tanya and I introduced ourselves.

'When I first saw it, I thought this place was a sort of abandoned house,' I said. 'It looks pretty cool, you have to admit.'

'Yeah, it must have been beautiful once. It used to belong to someone called Lady Teresa who owned loads of land around here,' said Tanya. 'Apparently she left it to her grandson when she died about twenty years ago and he lets the local council run our community centre there. It needs loads of renovation, but I don't think he has the money to pay for it. Dad said that the people who use it the most are worried about the work not being done.

If it gets much more dilapidated, it will have to be pulled down.'

'We've been going there since we were little,' said Frixos. 'Day care, then football, then music club. It'd be awful if it was gone!'

'We'd have to do something to stop it shutting,' said Sam, and I could hear the determination in his voice.

We soon arrived at the front door of Skipton House and Mr Chandler motioned for us to come in.

'Shoes off at the front door,' he announced.

Tanya rolled her eyes. 'Make sure you double-wash your tights after this,' she whispered to me.

Inside, the centre was bigger than I'd imagined. There was a porch, with a small reception area, and two huge rooms, as well as a staircase leading to another floor. I heard jazzy music coming from somewhere above our heads.

'I think they have dance lessons up there,' Tanya explained.

'OK, guys,' said Mr Chandler. 'Please write your name on the sheet here, leave your coats on the hooks to your right, and come through when you're done. Mrs Gupta's ready for us.'

'I hope she does something easy. I can't be bothered with any complicated stuff,' Tanya said as we queued. 'It's not as if I'm ever going to be making any *proper* food anyway. It's just a bit of fun, isn't it?'

'What? Why wouldn't you make proper food?'

She paused, as if really considering the question.

'I don't know. I guess I don't have to when Ana's there. She cooks the most delicious stuff. It's terrible when she goes on holiday. Even then she freezes us loads of meals to get us through.' But as she was talking, she looked over at me and suddenly seemed embarrassed by what she was saying. 'I suppose I *should* learn to cook,' she added.

'Ana does *all* your cooking?' I asked, shocked.

'Well... yeah. She's so good at it. Her feta cheese and honey filo parcels are absolutely to die for.'

'Wow, sounds awesome.'

'You should come round one day and try them,' she said, in a casual voice, as if it was the most normal thing in the world for her to be inviting me to her family mansion.

I imagined a huge house with neat flower beds on either side of a wide gravel driveway. It had marble columns and fruit trees growing in the front garden. I wondered whether Ana was their only member of 'staff' as they called it in the Victorian-style TV shows that Lara loved, or whether they had others.

'Watch out for the ingredients they'll be using here,' Tanya warned me, wrinkling up her nose.

'Gather round,' said Mrs Gupta, who was smiley, and wore a billowing floral-print dress. 'I wanted to welcome you, and also to say that if you're feeling tired after a full day of school, don't worry – this won't be like any of your lessons. For a start, we don't sit at desks and we rarely write anything, unless you're keen to jot down some of your favourite recipes. By far the best and the most important part of what we do – the "culinary magic" as I like to call it – happens in the prepping, the cooking and the baking. Hands up if you've never made a meal before?'

A sea of hands, including Tanya's, waved.

'OK. That's fine. It's what I expected. Don't worry, because by the end of today – you may not believe it – that will have changed. Some teachers will tell you that you need to understand the theory before you can actually master a particular skill, but I disagree. I think the best thing to do is to get stuck in. So today, we're going to make the most basic of dishes, but a super tasty one nonetheless – pancakes.'

An excited murmur went round the group.

'Now,' Mrs Gupta continued, rubbing her hands together with pleasure, 'as with any recipe, there are two important things to remember – the ingredients and the quantities. Does anybody know what ingredients we need for a good pancake?'

'Use the pancake mix from the supermarket,' Tanya whispered to me, winking. 'It comes pre-mixed.'

'Eggs,' said a boy at the front.

'Milk,' somebody else shouted out.

'Flour?'

'Exactly right. Well done, everyone. Plus a smidgen of oil, a pinch of salt and, of course, anything that you would like for your topping. An easy, traditional topping is lemon and sugar. But I think that people often forget that pancakes can be savoury too – they don't always have to be served as dessert.'

There were various toppings mentioned, from obvious ones like chopped bananas and chocolate spread to some weird and wonderful ones like chicken and spicy beans.

'I love melted cheese and spinach,' said Mrs Gupta. 'You might think it sounds disgusting, but I bet that you'll change your mind if you try it. It's a very tasty, inexpensive meal for lunch and dinner. My nephew, who's about your age, absolutely loves it.'

My ears pricked up at the word 'inexpensive' and I jotted down the recipe that Mrs Gupta was writing on the board. I'd made pancakes a couple of times with Lara for Pancake Day, but I'd forgotten the recipe, and I'd never really thought of them as something that you could have as a regular meal.

'OK, humour me. Let's do one batch of lemon and sugar, and one batch of my *pancakes a la Gupta*.'

We gathered around her cooking station where she showed us how she measured out each of the ingredients into a bowl.

'I'm going to use an electric whisk,' she said, taking out a white, two-pronged machine from one of her drawers, 'but I'm being lazy. You can totally mix these ingredients by hand.'

The mixture that she produced was a soft, creamy colour of just the right consistency, so that when she poured it into her frying pan, it made a satisfying sizzle.

'You'll know when it's ready to flip, because the edges will start curling. Now don't feel that you need to be one of those TV chef pros who flips perfect pancakes straight away. You can use a spatula to help you out. I still prefer to use it now, after years of making these.'

Then she sent us off to our own workstations in pairs to have a go ourselves. I basically had free rein over mine and Tanya's pancakes as she was too scared to touch anything.

'This time you go for it and I'll watch.'

I was delighted when the mixture ended up looking good. There were a few lumps which turned into black dots when I put the pancake in the pan, but otherwise, I was super pleased with my first two pancakes.

Then I carefully melted the cheese and wilted

the spinach in the same hot pan as we'd used for the pancakes. Even Tanya looked vaguely impressed.

'Here, one for you, one for me,' I told her.

'I told you not to eat this stuff,' she hissed but I was no longer listening. I cut myself a generous slice and raised it to my mouth. It was like a little puff of heaven – the gorgeous sweet and salty tastes mixed in my mouth and the texture of the gooey cheese was incredible. Before I knew it, the entire pancake was gone and Tanya was looking at me with a mixture of fascination and disgust.

Mrs Gupta's Spinach and Cheese Pancakes

Ingredients

- 100g plain flour
- 2 pinches of salt
- 2 eggs
- 300ml semi-skimmed milk
- 1 tablespoon sunflower or vegetable oil

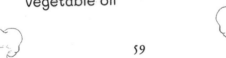

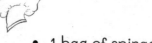
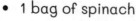
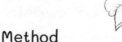

- 1 bag of spinach
- 50g cheddar cheese

Method

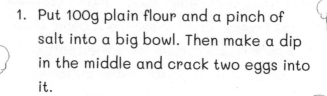

1. Put 100g plain flour and a pinch of salt into a big bowl. Then make a dip in the middle and crack two eggs into it.

2. Pour in about 50ml of milk and one tablespoon of sunflower oil and start whisking slowly — either using an electric whisk or a hand whisk. It can even be a spoon if you have nothing else. You should end up with a smooth, thick batter.

3. Keep adding the remaining milk, a bit at a time and stir until you have a nice runny consistency for pouring.

4. Heat a pan and add a small amount of oil. To get an even spread, you can use some kitchen paper. Pour some batter into the pan — it's great if you have

a pan with a lip, or use a big spoon to help. Tilt the pan around to get a smooth, even layer.

5. Here's the tricky bit. When the edges of the pancake are beginning to curl, take a flat spatula and flip it over. If you're feeling brave, skip the spatula and toss the pancake in the air using the pan, and the force of gravity.

6. Wilt the spinach by putting it in a pan and adding a pinch of salt — stir until the leaves turn soft. Meanwhile grate the cheddar cheese and sprinkle on top of the spinach, mixing it in to make the whole thing gooey.

7. Put a layer of cheesy spinach in the middle of each pancake and roll into a tube. Munch away!

At the front of the room, I saw that Frixos and Sam had taken great care over putting their ingredients together. It was only at the flipping stage, when Mrs Gupta's back was turned, that they went a bit wild, and one of the pancakes ended up temporarily stuck to the ceiling. It even caught Tanya's attention. When it slowly began to unstick, Frixos expertly caught it on his plate and began to tuck in.

'Gross,' said Tanya. 'He reminds me of my brother. That's exactly the kind of thing Jayden would do.'

'Right, everyone. Finish your pancakes, and it's clearing up time I'm afraid,' said Mrs Gupta clapping her hands. 'I hope I've piqued your interest and you'll come back next week. Hands up who enjoyed today?'

We raised our hands, and Sam even gave her a 'Whoop whoop!'

'Good. Well, I have a surprise for you next week, so make sure you're here.'

'Will you come again? Please?' I asked Tanya. I didn't want to sound desperate, but I needed a cooking partner, and if she didn't come I would be paired with someone random, maybe even from another year.

'Sure,' she shrugged. 'It's quite entertaining in a

weird way. Come outside with me? I need to wait for Ana to collect me.'

But then when we left the building, to my great surprise, there was Lara, chatting away to an older, red-haired lady.

'Erin, love!' She waved me over. 'I thought I'd come and see what this Cooking Club was all about.'

'Who's that?' asked Tanya. 'Your au pair?'

'What? No, my mum.'

Lara was wearing jeans and a baggy jumper, and with her hair up and no make-up, she looked even younger than she was. She gave Tanya a big grin when she saw her and introduced herself. But they couldn't chat for long, because Ana's car pulled up and Tanya jumped in.

'I was chatting to Mrs Rourke,' Lara said, beckoning me in the direction of the older lady. 'She lives round the corner from us. I think her grandson, Sam, is in your year.'

'Hiya, pet,' the lady said. 'You can call me Molly.' Her face was creased like a raisin, but she had bright blue eyes, which seemed to twinkle with delight. 'So you've not been to our Skipton before?'

'No, first time. It was a good club though.'

'My Sam comes for music breakfasts twice a week. Mind you, I don't think much proper music happens. It's mostly having a get-together, playing the guitar and singing a few songs, and they put on a breakfast too which helps. I used to take them in, but now he and his friend Frixos walk together, which I think is safe enough. You see, my arthritis—'

But she was cut off by the boys suddenly arriving by her side. Like Tanya, they looked at Lara with interest.

'Hi, I'm Erin's mum,' she said. 'We've recently moved here, so we haven't had a chance to meet you yet.' Frixos and Sam introduced themselves and we began to walk in the direction of home, the three of us a few steps behind Lara and Molly, who were deep in conversation.

'So tell us more about yourself,' said Frixos. 'Where are you from? What does your mum do? She seems pretty awesome.'

I ended up telling them about London, about

Lara losing her job, and even about the Cookathon. I later realised that maybe I wasn't supposed to have mentioned the last two things, but it was so easy to talk to them, maybe precisely because I didn't know them very well. I was sure that Lara hadn't heard me anyway.

'If you want to walk home from school together, we can wait for you outside,' Frixos offered as we said goodbye at the foot of the stairs.

'Sure. That'd be great. Where do you live?' I asked.

'A six-minute walk that way,' he said, pointing to the long road that wound off to the right at the intersection with Dunstan Row.

'And I live in that row of houses over there,' said Sam, 'at the end of the playing fields. You used to be able to cut through to get here, but now they've shut off access and we have to go the long way round.'

He was talking about the famous Alms Houses that Ali had mentioned that day at lunch and suddenly my impression of what they were like changed entirely.

'Well, it's great to meet you. I'd love to hang out,' I said.

So much had changed in a day. I suddenly had three friends and a great new club to go to – things didn't seem bad.

I ran into the flat feeling so happy that I forgot that tomorrow was The. Big. Day.

Seven

When we still lived on our old estate in North London, I liked to watch the sunrise from our little balcony. I sometimes went out there even in the middle of winter to get a few lungfuls of freezing, clear air. Sometimes dawn even in this grimy part of the city was so beautiful, that for a few moments, I forgot where I was.

Today, I ran out onto our balcony to watch Lara walk to the station. Even though I'd set my alarm, it turned out I'd missed her before she left the flat. I wished more than anything that I could go with her to the Cookathon. Instead, I grabbed my phone and sent her a message.

I was going to wish you luck but you don't need it. Your fajitas will be bellissimo! xx

I saw her pull her phone out of her bag to look at my text. She turned around and waved at me. Then I saw her typing something.

Haha, fingers crossed. I'll message as soon as it's over xx

I couldn't stop thinking about Lara throughout the first period of double maths.

Tanya must have seen how worried I was, because she mouthed, 'Are you OK?'

I nodded but carried on biting the skin around my fingernails.

'What's up?' she asked me at break. 'I can tell that something's wrong.' So I told her about Lara and the Cookathon, and about how freaked out I was by so many changes happening so quickly.

'Ah, that's where you get it from then!' she said, smiling.

'What?'

'Your love of cooking.'

'Yeah, I guess.'

'But you don't seem that happy about your mum wanting to become a chef,' she said. It was funny, but until she'd said that out loud, I didn't realise how badly I was worried about it.

'I'm scared that it will take her a while to start earning any proper money. We're using our savings now, but they'll run out soon, and if they do – we might have to move again.'

Tanya looked shocked.

'I'm sure it won't come to that. She'll need to apply to loads of places, but I'm sure that something will come up.'

'Thanks.'

'And hey, I bet judging events like the Cookathon takes ages. You won't hear from her until the end of the day. In the meantime, I'm going to try and take your mind off it.'

'How?'

'I'll think of something by lunchtime.'

But she was saved from having to come up with any ideas by Frixos and Sam who found us in the canteen at lunch and parked their trays opposite us. From the corner of my eye, I noticed Ali spotting them, and making a quick U-turn to eat lunch with somebody else. I'd also realised by now that Tanya wasn't that keen on hanging out with her.

'Hey, did you hear about Mrs Gupta?' Sam asked us.

'What about her?'

'The ambulance came for her earlier. One of the Year Eights said that she already looked pretty sick at breaktime.'

'Do you know what was wrong?'

'I have no idea. I hope she'll be OK. At least she's being looked after by people who know what they're doing.'

'I'm sure she will be,' I said. That's what people say in this sort of situation, isn't it, because they want everything to be OK, but the truth was that none of us knew what would happen.

'It's not good news for Skipton either, is it?' said Frixos, looking worried.

'What do you mean?' I asked. 'Are you thinking Cooking Club won't be able to go ahead without Mrs Gupta?'

'Yeah,' he replied, 'and if there's another club cancelled, there's even more of a reason to shut

Skipton down. I'm wondering if we should do something. Could we find out more about the owner? Maybe we could write to him and offer to help out with fundraising?'

I was excited about the idea of a special mission, but then we got distracted when Sam suddenly asked, 'Hey, has your mum done the Cookathon yet?' Our detective work would have to wait for another day.

'It's happening right now,' I said. 'I haven't heard from her yet, but I'll let you know.'

'Cool. She seems awesome, she deserves to win,' said Sam. 'My grandma was saying how nice she was.'

His words echoed in my head as I walked up the stairs to our flat after school. I hadn't heard from Lara, and by now I was certain that no word meant bad news. I opened the door to absolute silence. She wasn't home yet. I put my backpack in my room and went to make myself a cup of tea.

That's where I noticed the pizza box. Sitting there on the counter, along with a plate of crusts and a half-drunk bottle of wine. My stomach dropped to the floor. Lara had a thing about fast food – she always went on about how unhealthy it was (apart from our special Saturday orders from Thaisty of course.) At the same time, she admitted it was easy to be tempted! When I saw the pizza and wine, I knew that it could only mean one thing.

I checked the living room and saw her apron and rucksack on the sofa. Then I crept into her bedroom, where the curtains were drawn tight to block out the world. I made out her shape – curled up in the corner of her double bed. I lifted the duvet and crawled in, giving her a hug. Her shoulders shook, and I gently stroked her back.

Being here now, reminded me how much I missed sharing a room with her. In our old flat, we only had one bedroom.

My single bed had been next to the big bay window and the majority of the rest of the space was taken up by Lara's bed, which she'd inherited from Grandma and which I would sometimes clamber into when I was younger. Lara refused to swap the bed for a single. She said that it was the one luxury that she was allowed, and that she wouldn't be able to sleep if she couldn't spread out. We shared a big, Victorian-style wardrobe which was always overflowing with clothes which she'd bought with her staff discount at Rodrigo's: high-heeled boots, tights in daring colours, not to mention underwear and single socks. Among this artistic mess, my clothes, in the three drawers I'd allocated for myself, were always immaculately folded.

But when we moved to the new flat, Lara had offered me the bigger of the two bedrooms. 'You deserve some space of your own,' she'd said, beaming as she successfully put the finishing touches to my very own flatpack wardrobe. She was talented like that – putting together a wardrobe in less than an hour took skill.

'But you've got so much more stuff,' I'd protested.

'Ah, I'll manage somehow. It'll give me a reason to chuck out some of my old junk.'

So Lara moved into the small room, and I moved into the master bedroom, which had more space than I knew what to do with. I missed the conversations that we'd had before we fell asleep. They were about the silliest things, from the right way to tie a belt on a jumpsuit, to whether the Queen had any say about what she wanted for dinner. I missed Lara's snores in the middle of the night, which sounded like a kitten purring, and the weird 'boom boom' beat of her alarm clock which always went off at seven a.m.

In our new flat, she was on the other side of the hallway – a couple of metres away, exactly four and a half of my strides (I'd measured on the first day), but it may as well have been an ocean.

Now I lay next to her, breathing in her perfume – 'a beautiful mix of citrus, lavender and forest foliage,' she'd told me proudly when she'd bought it in the sale.

'I was eliminated,' she whispered, turning towards me. Her face was puffy and swollen, and her mascara had left back smudges on her cheeks.

'Hey, it doesn't m—'

'In the last round,' she cut me off. 'There were three rounds and I was eliminated at the final stage. I was almost there.'

I swallowed hard. I could imagine how furious and frustrated she must feel. It was difficult to turn this into a positive, but I tried.

'Hey – you got *so* close. Can you apply again?'

'Not for another year. Those are the rules. There are so many people wanting to get on the show that they have to be given a chance. Anyway, it doesn't matter what the rules are. The fact is that I'm not good enough.'

'For what it's worth, I think you're excellent.'

'I know, love, but you can't pay my wages,' she said miserably.

'I bet the judges were awful. Are they the same ones as in the live shows? What did they say?'

'Well, the two judges for this stage, Benny and Celestine, were actually really nice. It almost makes it worse. They liked the fajitas – they said they were full of flavour. It seemed that they enjoyed the starter too – I made salmon rolls in the end. But then I messed up the timings on the dessert. And Erin, there was so much choice. You should have seen the market – it was literally every fruit, vegetable, meat and fish under the sun. Loads I haven't even seen before.

'Some of the other contestants were picking out this fancy stuff and I was overwhelmed. I should have stuck to what I knew, but I ended up trying to make fig muffins and they didn't turn out right. They were soggy and embarrassing. The figs were overcooked and they were separating from the dough. You didn't even have to put them in your mouth to know that they were a disaster. I was burning with shame when I had to present them. I can't believe I'm such an idiot.'

'You're not an idiot. It's the first time you've ever done this kind of thing. No wonder it was stressful.'

'At least I found out early on, eh? So I didn't waste loads of our savings. Now I can start applying to some shops.'

I looked at her hot, sad face and it made me want to cry too out of frustration and rage.

Eight

Lara refused to get out of bed the following morning – even my French toast didn't help.

'I'm sorry, love, I should have said I wasn't hungry. It smells tasty though. You go and enjoy it. I'll stay here today. I need some time to think things through and digest everything that's happened. It's been such a whirlwind. I promise I'll be back to myself tomorrow.'

I tried to coax her out by saying it was Saturday, and wonderfully sunny outside, and that we could go window-shopping or for a walk by the river and play our favourite ever game – seeing how many dogs we could pet on the way. Lara nearly always won. She had a special smile that she always gave dog owners, and even the grumpiest ones caved and let her stroke or even hug their furry babies. Her unbeaten record in one walk along this stretch was twenty-two. I only ever managed sixteen even though I was definitely more of a dog-lover than she was. My greatest dream was to walk down this path with a dog of my very own. But this time even the prospect of loads of friendly, furry faces couldn't change Lara's mind.

In the end I brought her a cup of tea, left it by her bed and shut the door. On impulse I called Tanya.

'What are you up to?' I asked.

I think she could tell from the sound of my voice that something wasn't right, because she asked me straight away whether I would like to come round. She gave me her address, which I wrote on a piece of notepaper for Lara so she'd know where I was. I didn't want to disturb her in case she'd fallen asleep again. I knew that sometimes Lara's way of coping with sadness was to sleep through it.

It turned out that Tanya's house was about a twenty-minute walk from mine, but I didn't mind because it was gloriously sunny and felt more like the beginning of June than September. I took the riverside path and imagined what it would be like to walk here every day with a dog, its nose snuffling in the undergrowth, tail wagging with happiness. I'd wanted a dog as far back as I can remember, but we'd always lived in flats, and it would have been cruel to leave one on its own for hours, while I was at school and Lara at work. Plus, a dog was an additional cost, one which we couldn't afford right now. My dream would have to wait.

Tanya's house was big, with its own drive and roses in the front garden, but it was nothing like the grand mansion I'd expected. She opened the door almost as soon as I rang the bell.

'She didn't get in?' she asked, looking at my face.

'No.'

'OK, you have to tell me everything. But first – have you eaten? We're having a late breakfast – Dad went to get some croissants and scones from the bakery before work. There are loads left.'

She led me to a vast kitchen in which the entire back wall was a sliding glass door leading into the back garden. It gave the impression that we were practically eating outside and reminded me of the photos from travel magazines filled with holiday villas that I read at the dentist.

'This is Erin,' Tanya announced, 'Erin, this is Jayden and Ana.'

'It's lovely to meet you,' said Ana, who was a large, grey-haired lady with a fierce expression which turned out to be completely misleading, because when she smiled, warmth radiated from her. 'I hear you're the new friend who encouraged Tanya to go to Cooking Club. I'm so pleased.'

'Yes, it's actually surprisingly good,' I told her.

Jayden waved at me and went back to reading his comic.

'Help yourself,' said Tanya, indicating a big plate of pastries in the middle of the table. 'And there are strawberries too, and grapes.'

'Right, I'd better drive Jayden to his friend's birthday party. Will you girls be OK?' Ana asked us.

'Yeah, of course. I'm going to show Erin something and then maybe we'll take a walk up Willow Hill. What d'you think?' Tanya asked me.

'Great. I haven't been up there yet.'

So Tanya took me to her bedroom and opened a fancy-looking laptop. 'This is my dad's old one – he's letting me use it, but only for schoolwork,' she said. 'Look, I wanted to show you what my dad started up a few years ago – it has lots of helpful information about how to give yourself the best chance when you're applying for jobs. He was working with a charity then which supported the unemployed. But then it grew, and now lots of different people use it. Your mum might find something useful.'

'And it's free?'

'Yeah, that's something that Dad was always very certain about – it had to be free.'

'He sounds like an awesome person, your dad.'

'He is. I'm really proud of him,' she said quietly. 'When Mum died, he promised me and Jayden that he would always do his best for us – even when he was really upset and angry.'

'It must have been hard.'

'It was. But thanks to him, we somehow learned to cope, and then he found Ana to help us, which was fantastic.'

'She seems lovely.'

'She is. Anyway, have a look at this,' she said, angling the laptop towards me. She turned away, putting her hand to her eyes. I could tell that she was trying to stop herself crying and I gently put my arm around her shoulder.

The website was brilliantly laid out and I loved how easy it was to navigate between the different sections, even for people like us who had never applied for a job. As I was watching Tanya click through the different sections, an idea popped into my head.

'Do you think my mum could do something like this, except for cooking? She could store her recipes on a website and have little videos to show everyone how each dish is made? I read somewhere that if lots of people look at your website then advertisers will pay you money to help promote their products.'

'That's an awesome idea! Like a cooking blog? I think she should totally do it!'

'She has so many recipes already in her old notebook. So to start with she could copy those over!'

'Definitely. Come on, let's talk it through on the way up Willow Hill.'

It was the biggest hill in our new area, and I'd been wanting to go up there with Lara to admire the views, but we hadn't had the time. Today, the route was nearly empty. There were a couple of young mums with prams getting some exercise as they pushed their babies up the hill, and the occasional dog walker, but for most of the journey we were on our own.

The view of the town spread out to the left of us and in the distance I could make out our estate, and Skipton House.

'I have an idea about what to do to try and save Skipton,' said Tanya, as if reading my thoughts. 'I know it means so much to loads of people, not just Frixos and Sam.'

'Go on.'

'We need to start by finding out who the owner is. He keeps himself to himself and nobody even seems to know his name. So we need to be really careful in the way that we approach him.'

'How do you mean?'

'I'm still thinking it through, but I'll let you know when I have a plan. This will require some proper detective work.'

'I'm made for detective work,' I told her. 'Let's get together and figure it out.'

'We will, maybe even later today if we get a chance. But I've been meaning to ask you – what happened with the Cookathon?' Tanya said.

'Mum was close, but she messed up the dessert. She's so upset about it that she won't get out of bed,' I summarised.

'That's awful, I'm sorry,' said Tanya, pulling me into an unexpected side hug. 'It must be gutting for her, but she needs to try again. You believe she's good enough, right?'

'Yeah, she truly is. She's had so many years of practice. You know the recipe book I told you about? All the recipes in there are unique, not stuff that she's copied from someone else. They're dishes that she's perfected through trial and error and they have her personal twist. Some of the recipes even come with a little note, like a diary entry, on what inspired her to create it. And the best thing is, the ingredients are easy to find and they're cheap – it means anyone can make these meals. You don't have to be rich or go to special shops or anything.'

'That's awesome. It's actually what I really liked about Cooking Club – Mrs Gupta doesn't use anything expensive or fancy. If your mum's the same, I bet there will be loads of people who will want to cook her dishes. There are so many different ways of promoting her recipes through social media. And I remember Dad saying that some bloggers get loads of money through sponsorship and advertising. That's how he uses the recruitment blog to raise money for his charity.'

'I need to find out how to set one up for her,' I said, thinking aloud. We'd reached the top of Willow Hill and the huge, grand view of not just our town, but the whole surrounding area, stretched below us. The air was still, and the sky was so clear and bright, that the whole thing looked like a painting.

'This place is one of the best things about living here,' said Tanya. 'When we were younger, mine and Jayden's favourite game was coming here and seeing how many church spires we could count. I got up to eleven. Hey, can you see those guys over there? It looks like they've got a cage. What d'you reckon they're doing?'

And it was only when we got much closer that we saw it was Frixos and Sam. Frixos was holding a small cage and there was a fluttering sound coming from inside.

'Hey!' Frixos called, waving us over. 'Come and help us release Barry!'

It turned out that Barry was a pigeon which Sam had rescued from beneath a bush and nursed back to health.

'How do you know he's ready?' I asked.

'I don't, to be honest, we've had a couple of false starts. On Monday he started getting restless and that was my first attempt to release him, but he walked a short distance and then fell over, so I could see that it wasn't the right time yet. Then we had a second try on Wednesday after school. He even flew a little bit, but in the end he came back to me.'

'But today, we saw him strutting around in Sam's garden, and I could tell,' said Frixos proudly.

I noticed now how much louder he was than Sam. Sometimes it seemed as though he was doing the talking for both of them.

'Are you leaving him in there to prepare him for what's about to happen?' Tanya guessed.

'Yeah, I think I rushed him last time and that was a mistake,' said Sam quietly. 'You have to have a lot of patience with birds – it's about building trust. I think being at our place was good for him though. It's pretty peaceful.'

'The exact opposite of my house,' said Frixos, rolling his eyes. 'Hey, Erin, how did everything go with the Cookathon auditions?'

I groaned inwardly. I wished I hadn't told so many people.

'She didn't get through?' Sam asked.

I shook my head.

'I'm sorry. But in a way – it's kind of to be expected. It's only her first step.'

'How do you mean?' I was intrigued. Nobody I'd told had reacted this way.

'My grandma always says that a winner is a loser who tried one more time. It's rare for anyone to get where they want to be on their first attempt, particularly with little preparation. They would have to have the most incredible luck. And as with

87

anything, I bet there were things that affected whether or not your mum got through – like what judges were there on the day. Some of them would like particular dishes more than others. Or what she decided to cook. Or even whether she was feeling nervous or calm.'

'You're right,' I said, amazed that even though he didn't know much about the situation, he'd managed to get it spot on. I thought back to Lara's panicked selection of ingredients at the market.

The four of us sat on the grass. I closed my eyes and felt the wind on my face. I could hear the distant noise of a child laughing, the hum of traffic on the motorway, and Barry pecking at the cage bars. It was still so warm, even though the smell of autumn was in the air – earthy and sweet.

'She just needs support from the right people to try again,' said Sam after a while. 'Barry's had a few false starts, but he has us to help him back up, doesn't he?'

'Yeah. I'm going to do everything I can to help her.'

'Erin's actually had a great idea,' said Tanya.

'Are you ready to share it with them?' she asked excitedly.

So I told them about my plans for the blog, even though at this stage they were still vague.

'That's fantastic!' Frixos agreed. 'And after it's been up for a while and doing well, when people type a recipe into the search bar, your mum's will come up somewhere near the top of the listings. I know a bit about how it works, because Gabriel's been teaching me. He's my older brother. He's doing Computer Science at A level and he's hoping to do it at uni too.'

'D'you think he could help me to set up a blog?' I asked hopefully.

'For sure! He's always looking for real-life projects to practise on. You should meet him. In fact, why don't you two come for lunch?'

'I'd love to,' Tanya and I said at the same time.

'Great. We need to do the deed and then we can head over.'

I'd almost forgotten about the poor pigeon still in the cage wedged between Sam's legs. I crouched next to him.

'Are you ready?' Sam asked him.

Frixos swung the door open. I held my breath, expecting him to fly out immediately and make curious circles of the hilltop. But he was cautious. He took three tentative steps and then stood quietly.

'You've done a great job, you know,' Frixos told Sam. 'He looks like any other pigeon – you can't even tell that he had a broken leg.'

'I bet he'll miss you. I'm sure birds remember people who have helped them,' said Tanya, and as if on cue, Barry edged towards Sam and seemed to stare straight into his eyes. It was a gentle look, as if he was saying goodbye.

'Off you go,' Sam whispered. 'Go on, Barry. You're ready. Let's hope that the wind takes you to see your friends.'

The pigeon made a few attempts to launch himself from where he was standing, and when that failed, he broke the journey into several steps – first, he hopped onto a bush, then a nearby branch and finally up towards the top of a tree. It was clever, because the tree jutted over the edge of the hill, where the wind was the most powerful. He eventually stepped carefully off the highest branch and spread his wings wide.

We watched as he soared over the grassy ledges and streets below until he became a dark grey speck in a sea of green.

'He's a trooper,' I said. I loved that he hadn't given up, despite having failed twice.

'He is,' said Sam, and I couldn't be sure, but I thought that I heard his voice shake, ever so slightly.

Nine

'**R**ight, lunch,' said Frixos, shutting the empty cage. 'I'm supposed to be buying it for the masses because Mum and Dad are away. On weekends, lunch is our main meal of the day.'

'What are you making?' I asked the boys. 'Can I help?'

'Err... I was thinking of going to the chicken shop down the road and getting a couple of those family buckets. Either that or pizza.'

'Why only those two options?'

'Because I don't have that much cash,' said Frixos, looking slightly embarrassed. He dug his hand in his pocket and pulled out a crumpled ten pound note.

'What if we spent the money on ingredients and cook something?'

'Like what? There's no way that we would be

able to afford it. Not to fill up that many people anyway. There would be eight of us.'

'OK, what if I prove to you that you could?'

'Ah, she wants a challenge!' said Sam, rubbing his hands together. 'Frixos, let her do it.'

So we went to the supermarket, and the boys watched in awe as I bought ingredients for dinner which came to a total of £9.10. We laid them out in Frixos's kitchen and everyone helped me cook.

'Cool. So we're going to call this dish Frixos's Feast,' I said, 'because you're our host. It's a version of fish paella – a Portuguese dish that my mum likes to make.'

Tanya volunteered to stir the special rice as it soaked up the hot water. When we put the seafood in, a delicious smell filled the kitchen and sent Frixos's three younger sisters and older brother Gabriel running in. At first, I panicked that there wouldn't be enough food for everyone, but the rice expanded to about five times its size in the process of cooking and it turned out that there was loads of fish in the bag, so even when split into eight portions, there was plenty for everyone.

Frixos's Feast

Ingredients

- 1 tablespoon olive oil
- 1 onion, finely chopped
- 1 stock cube
- 500g paella rice
- 1 head of broccoli
- 1 bag of fresh peas
- 1 tablespoon saffron powder
- 1 bag of frozen seafood

Method

1. Heat the oil in a large frying pan. Add the chopped onion and stir until softened (about 5 minutes).

2. Prepare a large measuring jug of boiling water from the kettle (500ml) and stir in the stock cube until dissolved. Then tip the 500g of paella rice into the pan and immediately add about 100ml of the water, so

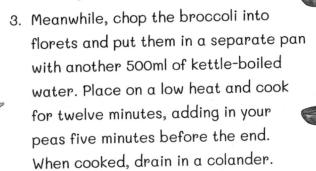

that it covers the rice completely. Keep adding the water bit by bit and stirring, until the rice soaks it up.

3. Meanwhile, chop the broccoli into florets and put them in a separate pan with another 500ml of kettle-boiled water. Place on a low heat and cook for twelve minutes, adding in your peas five minutes before the end. When cooked, drain in a colander.

4. Finally, stir in a tablespoon of saffron powder, then put the seafood mix into the pan and cover it with a lid. Simmer for 5 minutes until it is cooked through. Then add the vegetables and stir these in gently.

'This is delicious,' said Gabriel, tucking into his paella. 'Great work. Was this your idea?' he asked me.

'Yeah, I love to cook. Not as much as my mum though – she's the real cooking pro in our house.'

'I'm trying to get better,' said Frixos. 'I've been practising some of the Cooking Club recipes. I even made Mrs Gupta's pancakes the other day, and they turned out all right! At least – there weren't any complaints. They were eaten in about five minutes.'

Later, when Frixos's younger siblings were washing up, we went to his bedroom.

'Do you have a computer we could use?' asked Tanya. 'I wanted to look something up about Skipton.'

'Sure, Dad lets me borrow his. One sec.'

'What are you thinking?' asked Sam, as Frixos went to get his dad's laptop.

'I think I can figure out the name of Skipton's owner. First we need to find out more about Lady Teresa, his grandmother, who handed down the property to him in her will.'

'How do you know about her?' I asked.

'We were taught about her at primary school,' said Tanya. 'She did lots to support the local community. There's a statue of her in the high street, near the cinema. You must have seen it?'

'Oh, *that's* her. I didn't realise.' I'd seen the statue in town with Lara. It was a bronze one of an older lady sitting at a table.

Tanya typed 'Milwood, Lady Teresa' into the search engine to see what came up.

Lady Teresa Davenport (1899–1981), a local aristocrat and philanthropist. She famously gave away more than 80 per cent of her land to benefit the poor of the local community and to develop learning opportunities for children. The land she herself inherited stretches from the current Milwood Estate through to the left bank of the Longly River.

'That's her.' I scanned the rest of the text. 'But it doesn't say anything about her grandson. We can guess that his surname is Davenport, but what's his first name?'

Tanya typed in 'Davenport, Milwood.'

We came across a few more websites that mentioned Lady Teresa, but otherwise nothing.

'Hmm… this is tougher than I thought,' Tanya admitted.

'Hold on – look, there's a longer biography of her here,' I said, scanning a paragraph that popped up in a side column of the article Tanya was reading.

Lady Teresa's first marriage was to a headmaster of the local village school, Louis Wiley. They had one child together, Wilhelm, and remained married until Louis's death in 1950. At the age of sixty, Lady Teresa married into the Davenport family…

'So that means her grandson has a different surname to her. She wouldn't have had any other children from her second marriage, so Wilhelm must be the current Skipton owner's father.'

I quickly typed Wilhelm Wiley into the search engine and an article about 'Milwood Printworks' came up.

'Hey, those printworks still exist. They're near our school!' said Frixos. 'Maybe that's where we can find Wilhelm's son!'

'Hold on, look,' said Sam, scanning the article. 'It says here that Wilhelm Wiley opened the printworks in 1942, and handed them to his only son Edgar in his will, but Edgar sold them. That's the man we're looking for – Edgar Wiley! Now let's look *him* up.'

I did as Sam instructed, and several news items

came up, along with the website of the local technology business, where it turned out that Edgar was chairman. There was even a picture of him – a serious-looking man with a large nose and a head of thick, grey hair. Annoyingly, there was no email address or direct phone number for him anywhere.

'He looks like a reasonable person,' said Frixos, peering closely at the photo on the screen.

'How can you tell that just from looking at this?'

'Oh, I've always been really good at judging people's faces. Anyway, it looks like the only thing we can do is to write him a letter. We can print two copies and send one to Skipton House and the other to this company where he's chair, to make sure that he gets it.'

'But what do we say?' Sam asked. 'I feel like we can't be too obvious because he won't want to reply to us.'

'Exactly, we've got to leave it open and add a hint of mystery – keep him guessing.'

In the end we drafted the following:

Dear Mr Wiley,

We hope you're well. We're a group of students from the local area and we have some information regarding Skipton House which we wanted to share with you, and which we hope you will find valuable and interesting.

Would it be possible to arrange a short meeting with you? We're free every weekday from 3.30 p.m, except Thursdays.

We left our names at the bottom along with Frixos's email address and Tanya's mobile number.

'I have a good feeling about this,' said Tanya as we waited for the pages to print. 'I've got to head back now but I'll post them on the way home.'

'Great. Hey, Erin – before you go, do you want to ask Gabriel about your mum's website?'

'Yes, that would be awesome.' In our hunt for Skipton's owner, I'd almost forgotten about Lara's blog.

After Tanya left, we went to Gabriel's room. It was a tiny box room in the attic, but everything was neatly arranged. Books lined an entire wall above a small desk, and his bed took up the rest of the space. The three of us sat down on it in a row.

'Sorry to barge in. A quick question,' said Frixos.

'One sec, let me finish this.' Gabriel ran his finger down the page of the book he was holding, then entered a few numbers into a whole sequence of what looked like random numbers on his laptop, then closed it and turned towards us. On the front cover I noticed the title, *Python 3.8*.

'What are you doing?' I asked him, genuinely curious.

'Eh? Oh – you mean the code. I'm working on this website for my friend's dad. He's opening a restaurant and he was going to get an agency to design his website and pay them loads, so I said that I could do it for him instead. If I mess it up, he can still go with the agency, but he's giving me a chance. I wanted a real project to practise on for my A level and I reckon I'm not too bad.'

'He's being modest. He's excellent,' said Frixos.

'There's loads of tools online that give you website templates, so it's not as if it's rocket science,' he said.

'I actually wanted to ask for your help, because I'd like to start a cooking blog for my mum. How long does it usually take to create a basic website?'

'It depends how basic really. With an existing online template I reckon you could do it in a day or two. If you wanted some fancier extras, it might be a fair bit longer.'

'I think it needs to have a homepage with some information about her, and then a series of posts where she could put her recipes, maybe with some photos. She's got a whole exercise book of recipes at home and I could start her off with copying a few over onto the site.'

'Maybe she could post videos of herself cooking,' said Sam. 'Sometimes you need something like that to help you understand how to make stuff.'

'That might need some extra coding to embed it,' said Gabriel. 'But I reckon I could do it. If you wanted to get started on the blog, I could see if we can set you up right now.'

So we spent the next couple of hours crowded around Gabriel's laptop, peering at the screen as he created the first version of what would become Lara's website.

I forwarded him the photos that I'd taken of her for the Cookathon audition, and he arranged them on various pages, making the colours even more vibrant and eye-catching. I couldn't believe how fast it was coming to life!

'What do you want to call it?' he asked.

'Bellissimo Cooking for now,' I told him. 'We can always change it later.'

I wondered what name Lara would like. I couldn't wait to show it to her!

'Hey, that's actually a great name. Where did you get that from?'

'It's our surname,' I told him proudly. The more I said it in my head, the more it sounded like a unique and memorable name.

Gabriel showed me how to set up a password to get into what he called the 'back end' of the website, and we even tried creating a page with the first recipe which was, of course, for 'Lara's Fantabulous Fajitas'.

'Thank you. It means so much to me.'

'My pleasure. If you need any more help, come round. It helps me to learn stuff too.'

By the time Sam and I were walking home, it was almost evening.

'Thanks for teaching us how to make paella,' he said. 'It was really good. And I didn't realise how cheap it was to buy the stuff you need for it. I'll tell my grandma. She worries a lot about how much our shopping costs.'

'I'm glad you liked it. And thanks for what you said about Mum – you know, that it's only her first attempt. I think we forgot for a while that this is not the end of the road. I need to encourage her to keep going. Anyway, she seems to get on really well with your grandma. Tell me more about her – is it the two of you at home?'

'I live with her and my mum, but Mum's hardly ever home. She works long hours because she does two jobs back to back, so she often doesn't get in until nine p.m. Most of the time it feels like it's just me and Grandma. She's lovely but she's changed recently. She was always cheerful, but she's so worried about everything now. Her arthritis has got worse, which means she can't work any more and it's made her even more anxious than usual about money. I think she feels bad that my mum is the only one going out to work.'

And then he looked at me as though he wanted to say something else, but couldn't bring himself to.

'That must be tough.'

'Yeah, it's pretty hard, especially when she gets flare ups, and she can't really do anything for herself. She needs constant help then, and I'm scared to leave her on her own. But she's been prescribed some new medication now and well... we're hoping it will help. I haven't really told anyone apart from Frixos.'

'Don't worry, I won't mention it to anyone. I promise.'

'Thanks.'

'And also – I know what it's like to worry about spending. Mum's worried too now that she's lost her job, and it makes me scared sometimes. I hope she'll find something new soon, but we don't know when that will be. There's always people who can help though, Sam.'

'I know. But no one likes asking, do they?'

Ten

When I got home that evening, Lara was on a video call with Aunty Sarah in Sydney, who looked like she'd got up particularly early. Recently, she was being kept up at night by her newborn baby, my cousin Mia, so she rarely had time to chat. I know that Lara missed her. I heard her reassuring voice coming through the laptop speaker.

'You're going to be OK, you know,' Aunty Sarah said, 'because of two things – you're talented and you're strong. You don't believe it now, but you'll find a job which you love. I have a feeling it will be related to cooking.'

'I hope you're right. Maybe it's selfish, but it's what I've always wanted.'

'It's not selfish.'

That was when Lara spotted me out of the corner of her eye and called me over to look at the screen.

Aunty Sarah showed us baby Mia asleep and she asked me about school. When we finished the call, I gave Lara a big hug. I offered to make us some pasta, and then we sat down together to watch telly.

When I went to bed, I felt infinitely more hopeful than I had the night before, and I decided that tomorrow I would tell Lara my idea for the blog.

She got up early on Sunday and made us breakfast, which was a good sign, and I decided that I couldn't keep my idea to myself any longer.

'I have something to show you,' I announced. 'Can I borrow your laptop?'

'Sure. As long as it's not a job ad, love. I don't think I can quite face it yet.'

'No, don't worry – it's not a job ad. It's something far, far better.'

I made sure that she couldn't see my screen, as I loaded the page Gabriel had set up and logged into the area which allowed me to edit the text. Then, when I was sure I had her complete attention, I turned the screen around to show her.

'Oh my goodness, what is it?'

'Good question. It's the beginning of something that could become your website!'

'My website? Seriously? But... how did you do this? You're brilliant!'

'I have my talents... but they don't stretch to designing websites,' I laughed. 'This was done by Frixos's older brother, Gabriel. He managed to put this together in an hour and a half, and that's only using a basic template online. There's loads more that can be done with it if you like it. Look, we put in your photos, and there's a space for you to write about yourself, and I've even put in your first recipe on the blog page, although I think you'll have to correct it because I was typing quickly and I'm pretty sure I made some mistakes.'

Lara flicked through the different tabs, and I could see an expression of wonder return to her face.

'But it must have been you who came up with the idea?'

'Yes, but it was after seeing a different website that Tanya showed me, so you could say it was kind of a team effort.'

'It sounds like you've got a great gang of friends. It's so lovely of you to do this for me. I really appreciate it.'

'You don't have to do anything with it,' I said. 'You don't even have to make it live. I thought it could be a nice place to put your recipes, because I keep worrying that they'll get lost in that book of yours, plus – sometimes it's hard even for me to read your writing.'

'Oi! It's not that bad!' she said, but she was smiling. That's when I could breathe a sigh of relief, because I could see some of Lara's spark was back.

I showed her how to log in and use the site, and we copied over another couple of recipes from her book.

'This is a pretty special book,' I said, patting its battered cover.

'I suppose it is. But not just because of the recipes. You know, it's yours really. I was going to wait until it was full and I wanted to cover it in some nice paper before I gave it to you, but you've already read so many of the recipes, so consider it "a gift in progress".'

'Honestly? It's for me?' I couldn't believe what I was hearing. I'd always known the recipe book was one of Lara's most prized possessions.

'Of course. And to prove that it's true, you can read some of the diary entries.'

'Wow, thanks so much. I actually love it the way it is. You don't have to give it a new cover. The stains and smudges show the journey it's been on. It would be strange to have a clean recipe book.'

So later that afternoon, I spent some time copying over more of the recipes for her. And that was when, for the first time, I started properly reading it, not just following the recipes. It led me to a very important discovery.

The first diary entry that I came across was before the recipe for egglets:

 1st May 2009

I made a big batch of this today, because I am feeling incredibly hungry. And there is a good reason for it, because last week I found out that I'm going to have a baby!

I'm over the moon and scared at the same time, so much so that I couldn't really eat for the first few days after I found out, but I sat down with Sarah and she talked me through everything and calmed me down.

It's going to be difficult, because I've broken up with Mark — I'm not sure how involved he'll want to be, but I'm feeling strong, and I reckon I'll be able to do this on my own. I'll have to look for a place to live soon, because I won't be able to carry on renting here with Sarah and May once the baby comes, but that's still a way from now. Maybe I'll move back in with Mum?

I already know one thing for certain about my future little girl or boy — they absolutely love egglets. I wonder if that's something that will remain their favourite food? I'm excited to find out. Being pregnant has inspired me to start this notebook, which one day I want to give to him or her — my little Bellissimo!

I could feel a lump in my throat as I read, and frantically turned the pages to find more. There were a few short extracts in which Lara talked about how she was feeling or why she loved a particular dish, but it wasn't until August that I found another, longer entry:

 3rd August 2009

It's scorching today. The city is positively melting. Sarah showed me the footprints that she made in the asphalt in front of our house. It's a difficult time to be pregnant. None of my old jeans fit any more.

Rodrigo gave me a bonus last week, as it has been our best sales period since he first opened the shop. I decided to save most of it for when the baby comes, but I thought I would treat Mum to a nice lunch,

as we never go out. So we went to a fab
new brasserie that I'd heard a lot about
called Lily's.

They do basic dishes but with a twist,
always adding their own touches. When
I go to cooking school, I'd love to do my
work experience somewhere like this. I've
had to defer my place for September, but
I'm determined that I'll get there at some
point in the future. Mum even said that
some of the dishes at Lily's (I think she
meant the savoury pancakes in particular)
are no better than mine.

I keep thinking the baby will be a girl and
I hope that she loves food as much as I do.
Sometimes I can imagine her standing next
to me, helping to mix ingredients. I want
to show her that even if you don't have
much, you can make something special and
tasty for the people you love, if you only
know how to go about it.

Her recipe book is shaping up nicely!
(Haha, after all that, it will be funny if the
baby is a boy!)

About halfway through reading that second extract,
I realised I was crying – huge, round tears of relief
were trickling down my cheeks and nestling on
the collar of my denim shirt. *Being pregnant has
inspired me to start this notebook*, Lara had written,
and she'd been looking forward to meeting me so
much. I saved the rest of the entries for another day.
For now, this was plenty enough to melt away any
guilt I felt and for the first time in ages, I went to
bed feeling completely happy.

Eleven

Over the next couple of weeks Lara's blog rapidly grew – she was adding about three recipes a day and posting mouth-watering photos on Instagram. I think even she was surprised by the number of followers she was getting. I hadn't seen her look forward to anything so much in years.

Meanwhile, we still hadn't received a response from Edgar and the boys were considering going to the offices of the company, where he was chairman, to somehow request a meeting in person. Tanya and I thought it was a bad idea. We imagined he was busy and even if he happened to be there, he would probably turn us away on the spot.

'Let's wait another week,' we told them. 'He probably has a whole pile of letters to get through and hasn't got round to ours yet.'

But we were beginning to realise that time was something we didn't have much of, because one Tuesday lunchtime, Sam told us, 'I think Cooking Club is going to be cancelled.'

'What? Seriously? Why?'

'Mrs Gupta's not well again, and now she's not coming back until after her baby's born. I overheard Mr Chandler telling Miss Day in the staffroom.'

'What baby?' I asked.

'She's pregnant. We only recently found out. I think that time the ambulance took her, they were worried that there was something wrong with the baby. Then everything turned out to be OK and she was feeling better so she came back to work. But now she's taken another turn for the worse.'

'Maybe they've put her on bed rest?' said Tanya. 'Sometimes doctors tell women to stay in bed to keep them and the baby safe.'

'I hope she's OK,' I said. 'But now Mr Chandler knows for certain that she's not coming back, couldn't he find somebody else to run it?'

'Yes – he said that he'd put up a notice in the

staffroom to see if anyone was up for it. Miss Day said that she would love to do it, but she can't cook to save her life.'

'I'm gutted,' said Tanya. 'I know I wasn't sure about it to begin with, but now I'm going to really miss it.'

We'd only had three sessions of the club in total, but in that time, aside from the delicious savoury pancakes, we'd also managed to make an awesome carrot and tomato soup, chicken curry and an incredible apricot upside-down tart. We'd started to look forward to our weekly gatherings at the community centre and I longed to practise the new recipes at home.

'That's not everything,' said Sam glumly. That was when he dropped the real bombshell that made my stomach drop. 'My grandma says that Skipton House might be getting sold.'

'What? Are you serious? How does she know?'

'She's friends with Margaret, who works in the management team at Skipton. It might be rumours, but it might not be...'

'That's terrible. We can't keep waiting for Edgar

to respond. We need to act faster!' I insisted. 'Can we find out who's buying it?'

'I don't know. I'll ask Grandma. I suppose for now, nothing's confirmed. I'll check with her tonight to see if she knows anything else.'

'We need to show everyone how much it means to us. For a start, we need to think of a way to keep Cooking Club going,' said Frixos.

'Couldn't your mum take it over?' Tanya asked me, just as I was thinking exactly the same thing.

'I could ask her, but doesn't it have to be someone from school?'

'I don't know, maybe not,' said Frixos. 'Why don't we find out?'

So when Mr Chandler made the official announcement about it during form period that afternoon, I went up to him before the end of the day to ask. He seemed surprised and relieved.

'You think your mum would be keen to do it? If she is, I think we could make it work. I'd have to speak to the organisers at Skipton, but I don't see why not. I would still take you over there and stay for the duration of the club.'

That afternoon, I came home to find Lara working on her laptop.

'I've gone through almost forty recipes and edited them so they're easier to read. I've uploaded tons of photos and now I'm working on the videos. It's a big job though, Erin,' she sighed, as I helped myself to a cup of tea. 'I never realised how difficult it is to record films of yourself. I can position my phone on that middle shelf in the kitchen and press record. But I've had to do at least three or four takes for some, because I got nervous and started babbling, or I accidentally missed a crucial step of the recipe. And then I've had to cut a lot down, because I realised that they were far too long. It's taken me ages, and the irony is that I've forgotten to eat!'

'I think you need a break – and it so happens that I have a plan.'

'What kind of plan?' Lara asked, raising an eyebrow.

'Well, I wondered if you might want to run Cooking Club? Mrs Gupta can't do it any more, at least not until after her maternity leave, and that's months away.'

'Oh wow! Thank you for thinking of me. I would love to do it! But do you think I'd be any good? I've never done anything like that before.'

'But you've taught me how to cook, and now you've done video tutorials for huge groups of people.'

'I know,' she said, laughing, 'but they don't answer back, do they?'

'But we're such a friendly group. There's nobody mean and I think you'd really enjoy it.'

'Well... I suppose it would be nice to get out of the house. I've missed seeing people, and I've especially missed hanging out with you, love. I'm sorry – this blog has taken over my world. It's so *exciting* – all the interest I'm getting, but at the same time I realise that it's eaten into the time that we would normally spend together, and I wanted to get some of that back. I also wanted to thank you properly for your help in getting me this far and so... I have a surprise for you. There's somebody that I would like you to meet. I reckon you'll love him. And he's definitely excited to meet you.'

'Who is it?'

'You're going to have to wait until Saturday to find out. We'll need to travel over to him on the bus – it's about a twenty minute journey.'

'You won't tell me anything? You won't even give me a clue?'

She made the motion of zipping her lips shut and grinning at me.

That Thursday, we were so excited that Cooking Club was back on, and Lara posted about it on her blog and social media channels.

In the first session she got us to make our own pizzas, which we'd only done once before at home.

As we got into it, I remembered how easy it was – much, much simpler than it looked. The secret is making sure the base is exactly right. Even Tanya got stuck in, kneading the dough, and she was the first to dig in when we finished, but only after she'd taken some artistic photos of her food and sent them to Lara for her blog. I also snapped a few pics of Lara in action.

'Someone's changed their mind about eating what we've made,' I said, laughing.

'Haha, it smells so good, doesn't it?' she said wiping her cheek with a floury hand.

The boys loaded as much cheese as they could onto their pizza, mixing mozzarella, cheddar and even some parmesan that they found in the fridge. When they cut it into slices after taking it out of the oven, the melted cheese looped into huge strings which they tried to karate chop.

The awesome thing was that everyone's pizza was slightly different, and Lara recommended loads of other toppings to try at home.

Perfect Pizza

Ingredients

For the base

- 300g bread flour
- 1 teaspoon instant yeast
- 1 teaspoon salt
- 1 tablespoon olive oil, plus extra for drizzling

For the topping

- 100ml passata
- 1 crushed garlic clove
- 1 ball of mozzarella
- 50g cheddar cheese, grated
- A handful of halved cherry tomatoes
- Sliced ham or salami

Method

1. Start by making the dough for the base. Put the flour into a large bowl, then stir in the yeast and salt. Make a little well in the middle and pour in 200ml warm water and the olive oil. Then mix everything together with your hands or a spoon until you have a soft dough.

2. Sprinkle flour on the tabletop and knead the dough until it's smooth. Then cover it with a dishcloth and set it aside for 20 minutes.

3. Split the dough into two balls and then,

on a floured tabletop, use a rolling pin to make two large thin circular bases. Carefully lift them onto two baking sheets.

4. Heat the oven to 220°C. Mix the passata with the crushed garlic then spread it over the bases with a spoon.

5. Cut the mozzarella into slices and arrange them over the top of each base. Sprinkle cheddar cheese on top and add the halved cherry tomatoes all over. Add the ham or salami and any other toppings.

6. Put one pizza, still on its baking sheet, on the top shelf of the oven. Bake for 8 to 10 minutes until crisp. Repeat for remaining pizza.

When the club had finished, Lara and I waited for everyone to go home, and I heard them telling their parents what a good session it had been.

'See,' I whispered to Lara, 'I told you that you're amazing.'

Twelve

My happy bubble was burst in an instant on Friday lunchtime, when Sam confirmed the news about the sale of Skipton.

'It's official. My grandma heard from her friend at the council that the sale is going to go through at the end of September. We've run out of time.' His eyes looked tired and red-rimmed. I wondered whether he'd been up at night worrying about it.

'Hey, if the sale hasn't gone through *yet*, we can still stop it!' said Frixos. 'The way I see it, we have two options. We can keep trying to get Edgar to meet us and then persuade him not to go ahead with the sale by showing him how much the community centre means to all of us, or we could find out who's buying it and persuade them that we need the place more than they do.'

'My suspicion is that Edgar will be difficult to pin down – he seems like an extremely private person and the fact that he hasn't responded to our letter shows that he's either busy or not interested. I feel like we'll have more luck with tracking down the buyer,' I said.

'You're right,' Frixos agreed. 'But how do we even begin drawing up a shortlist of who the potential buyers could be?'

'Let's start with a brainstorm,' I said, pulling out my notebook from my rucksack and opening it on the middle page spread. *Suspect buyers* I wrote in the middle and surrounded it with a jaggedy bubble. 'Think widely. Do you know of anyone who might want to buy Skipton for any reason?'

'Ali's aunt owns lots of properties,' said Tanya. 'Well, they're more like bed and breakfasts in pretty locations. She has three so far and she always said that she wanted to expand it into "an empire". We stayed in one once back when we were still... Anyway, maybe she's bought Skipton to change it into another one of her B&Bs?'

I carefully noted down what Tanya had said.

'Anyone have anything else?'

'I think there's a high chance that it's a property developer,' said Frixos. 'More and more people are moving out here, because it's green, spacious and quiet, and it's still easy to get into the city. I've seen loads of new developments when I've been out on my bike. I'm pretty sure it's the same company – they're called something like Morton Villas or Villa Morton. They've probably bought Skipton House, and the land, and they'll be planning a whole new estate there.'

I had to admit that this was a strong lead, so I asked Frixos to check the name of the company and to find the details of their headquarters. Meanwhile I wrote *property developer* in a big bubble.

'Any other ideas?'

There was a silence while we thought hard. I suddenly realised that Sam hadn't said anything since he'd first told the gang the news. His fists were pressed against his cheeks and he was staring at the table.

'Are you all right?' I asked him.

'Yeah, fine,' he muttered. 'Nothing else comes to mind.'

'OK, let's keep thinking about any other potential suspects. In the meantime, we have two pretty strong leads, which we need to start investigating as soon as possible.'

'Yes, our mission begins. We should give ourselves a name. How about the Super Skipton Savers?' said Tanya.

'Nah, we need to sound more undercover and sly. More like the Cunning, Crafty Cooks,' said Frixos.

'Or maybe the Cooking Club Detectives?' said Sam, shrugging.

We looked at each other and nodded.

'I love it,' I said. 'Awesome.' I wrote the name down in my notebook above the two main suspects. 'So who do you think we should investigate first?'

'We have the most information on Ali's aunt, don't we?' said Tanya. 'She's called Arabella Snowstorm – it's easy to remember because it's so weird. Anyway, I can do some investigation online today to see if she has anything on her website about a new place opening. And if I can't find anything, we can always go to one of her B&Bs and do some snooping. The one we stayed in is actually really close – you can get there on the number fifteen bus.'

'Great. Let's use the coming week to collect information and we can do a detailed investigation of our suspects next weekend. Is everyone free then?' I asked.

'My cousins are coming to visit on Saturday,' said Frixos, 'but Sunday's OK for me.'

'I'm pretty sure I'm free,' said Sam, 'if... well...' he started and then stopped.

'If what?'

'If it's OK with my grandma,' he said eventually.

'I'm free,' said Tanya.

'OK, let's agree to split up,' I said. 'I'll go on Saturday with Sam and Tanya to the B&B and I'm sure we'll have other leads to follow up on Sunday.'

Frixos was staying at school a little later to wait for Gabriel who was taking part in a sixth form coding challenge, so Sam and I walked home, just the two of us.

'You said you were fine in the lunchroom, but I don't believe you,' I said when we got to the main road.

'Was it that obvious?'

'You don't have to tell me. But I wanted to say that I'm here in case you do.'

We walked in silence for a few minutes and then eventually he said, 'You know, I've been going to Skipton since I was a little kid. Then there was football and film society, and music breakfasts, and cooking club and judo. I can't really imagine all of that suddenly disappearing.

'But what's even scarier, is that I reckon Frixos is right. It's most likely some property developer who wants to build a big estate and before you know it, they'll want to expand, and you know what will be next to go?'

'What?'

'The Alms Houses, my home.'

His voice was shaking. We were almost at the field, and I pulled him into a hug.

I saw a bench on the other side of the hedge and gently led Sam over to it. I'd never noticed it before, probably because it was half-hidden by the shrubbery, but sitting on it gave you a beautiful view. There was a little flower garden at the edge of the field that led to Skipton House and all the autumn crocuses and dahlias had come out. Some of the irises were also beginning to bud – their little purple heads were already visible among the leaves. I'd learned lots of flower names from another of Grandma's books. I was amazed to find how many autumn 'budders' there were – before I'd always imagined flowers only bloomed in the spring.

'It's Grandpa's bench,' said Sam quietly.

'*Your* grandpa's?'

'Yeah – look.' He turned to show me the plaque attached to the back of it.

In memory of Joe O'Rourke,
who loved this place.

'This field is where Grandma and Grandpa first saw each other. They used to have barn dances here years and years ago, and that's how they met. They ended up getting married and having my mum, and Grandma always says how happy they were, even though it sounds like they were never very well off. Grandpa died about ten years ago now, when I was around two, but Grandma is always talking about him, so I kind of feel as though I know him. Does that sound weird?'

'No, of course not,' I said, holding Sam's hand tightly.

'It's fine,' said Sam, looking at me with an expression that implied he didn't want any sympathy. 'I'm sad for Grandma mainly. She used to be like a mountain – so calm and steady, and always protecting everyone. And she helped out a lot looking after me when my parents got divorced and my dad moved away. She and Mum made their jobs work around looking after me, and when they couldn't they took me to the day care centre at Skipton. I remember that when my mum's pay was delayed once, we had to use the food bank there, and the women who managed it were so kind. I loved it.'

'That's really sad about your grandma, but it sounds like you're already doing so much to help.'

'I don't know if I am. Luckily she still has lots of good days, but when she gets a bad flare up, she can't even move from the sofa. I wish I could do more for her, because she's done so much for me. D'you know what she always says when her friends tell her what a great job she and my mum have done bringing me up?' he asked.

'Go on.'

'She says they were able to do it, because they're part of such a supportive community. I'm sure that she mainly means the people who have worked at Skipton over the years. And the thing that I really don't want is for her to have to leave her home – if it turns out that this new development has plans for expanding. I have no idea where we would have to move to, but we wouldn't be able to afford any of these new flats that are being built, so it would have to be quite far out.'

'Oh Sam, we're going to do everything we can so that it doesn't come to that. I promise you. And whenever you want to talk, you know I'm always here.'

'Thanks.'

'Do you want to come and hang out with me at ours? We're making chicken salad with a twist. Come on, I'll show you. It always cheers me up.'

'OK. I'll let my grandma know that I'll be a little late.'

So that evening, we went to the shops and made Lara's chicken salad, which is one of my absolute favourites. Lara added avocado to it, which gave it a delicious, smooth taste.

Cheerful Chicken Salad

Ingredients

- 4 chicken thighs (boneless)
- 2 ripe tomatoes
- 2 stalks of celery
- 2 gem lettuces
- 1 bunch of grapes
- 1 avocado, cut into cubes
- 3 tablespoons mayonnaise
- 3 teaspoons milk

Method

1. Rub a small amount of olive oil into the chicken thighs, sprinkle with a pinch of salt and place on a lined baking tray. Cook them in the oven at 200°C for 15 to 20 minutes until the skin on top is golden.

2. Meanwhile prepare the salad. Dice the tomatoes and celery, pull apart the leaves of the gem lettuces and cut the grapes in half. Place all of these in a large bowl with the avocado cubes and mix together.

3. Next, prepare the dressing. In a bowl mix the mayonnaise and milk with a quarter of a teaspoon of salt and a pinch of black pepper.

4. When the chicken thighs are cooked, place them on the side and leave to cool for ten minutes. Then chop the meat into bite-size pieces, mix with the salad and add a generous helping of dressing.

'This is *so* good,' said Sam, tucking in.

'And so easy, right?' asked Lara, who'd joined us to eat.

'I'm definitely going to try and do it myself.'

'I'll give you the recipe. Try making it with your grandma. Look, we've even got some leftover chicken you can use.'

When he left to go home, I whispered to him by the door, 'We'll solve the mystery, you know. It's not over.'

'I know,' he said, and he sounded confident for the first time since I'd met him.

Thirteen

By the time Saturday morning came, I was dying to find out what Lara's surprise was. When I'd told the gang about it earlier in the week, everyone had a different theory. I thought that maybe some famous chef had been in touch with her on the blog and wanted to meet in person. Tanya thought it could be a model or some other celebrity who wanted to appear in Lara's cooking videos.

'Maybe it's that new guy on TV – you know, the one who's been doing the cooking show with those footballers?' said Frixos.

I'd tried to subtly get Lara to reveal more information about the surprise, but she wasn't giving anything away. She'd even cleared her search history on her laptop, as if she was expecting that I would do some snooping.

'Ready?' she asked, pulling on her sunglasses, as we walked to the bus stop.

'Absolutely.'

It was a particularly sunny autumn day – perfect for a postcard or a painting. There were conkers on the ground, and people milling around in the field behind our block, a group playing football. In the distance, Skipton House looked like a place from another time. I wondered if there were any classes held there on weekends.

The bus took us down the high street and north, out of town. It was my first chance to see parts of Milwood that weren't on route to school or the shops. We passed the little bookshop with the potted palm trees outside it that I'd heard about from Tanya, and a new-looking restaurant with a sign saying, *Big Venice*. A woman with bright red hair was standing in the doorway welcoming people. It made me think that it could be Lara one day.

We passed more playing fields, a fruit farm and an old, Victorian-looking school with a weird bell tower. I was still looking at this, when Lara told me we were getting off. Her phone told her to walk left and we suddenly found ourselves in a residential street of identical terraced houses.

'This is the one – red door,' Lara announced.

'I can't believe that anyone famous lives here,' I said.

And then Lara rang the doorbell and I heard a bark. A middle-aged lady with blonde hair opened the door. She reminded me of Grandma, or how I imagined Grandma in my head. She smiled at us and at that moment, a little dog's head appeared from behind her leg.

'Hey, there you are, little guy. I told him that you were coming, and I actually think he understood, you know. He got so excited. But come in, come in.'

I was so confused; I didn't even pay the dog any attention at first. I spent the whole time looking at the lady, trying to find out if she was in some way famous.

'We're here to see *him*,' said Lara laughing, pointing at the puppy, who started running excitedly around my legs.

'What? Oh, he's gorgeous!'

He was a lovely golden colour, and looked like he could be a cross between a Labrador and a dachshund. I'd never seen a dog in real life who looked quite so perfect.

'What breed is he?' I asked.

'Everyone asks that,' the lady said, laughing. 'He's a mongrel. His mum is definitely a Labrador, because she's my daughter's dog, but we're not sure about the dad. I'm guessing he must have been a smaller dog, judging by this little chap's legs.'

'What's his name?' I asked the lady.

'Well, that's up to you.'

'Up to me?' I asked, not understanding.

'He's yours,' said Lara grinning. 'He's your surprise.'

'What? Honestly? He's coming home with us?' I said, not believing what I was hearing. A bubble of joy started to form in the pit of my stomach.

'He's absolutely, fully and totally yours. There were three in the litter. My daughter managed to give the other two to her friends, but when this guy didn't get a home, I agreed to take him in for a while. We would love to keep him, but my husband is allergic.'

'So I saw the advert on a Facebook group and I read it and thought of you,' Lara finished triumphantly.

'He's beautiful,' I said, rubbing his ears. The dog looked at me, put one paw on each of my knees and sniffed me carefully.

'He seems to like you. Believe me, he's not like that with everyone. Look at his eyes,' she went on, 'who could say no to those eyes? He's a gorgeous little furry sausage.'

'Sausage,' I said to him, 'there's no better name for you.'

He barked and jumped up at me again, as if in agreement.

'I take it you want him?' asked Lara laughing.

'*So* much!'

I squeezed her tightly to say thank you.

It was the first weekend in absolutely ages that we did no cooking whatsoever, because we were so in love with our new housemate. We went for a long walk by the river in which Sausage made friends with the neighbourhood dogs. He sniffed them and tried to rub noses with the ones that he particularly liked.

And then as we walked the short distance home through the field, I saw my elongated shadow next to Sausage's little one and I felt madly happy. It had been a crisp and bright autumn day, and the sun was setting over the playing fields, a blaze of orange against the darkening sky. I wished that I could take a snapshot of this moment and store it for ever – not just a photo, but everything that went with it – the happiness, the quiet and the anticipation of an excited Sausage. My very own dog.

Fourteen

The more I got to know Sausage, the more I realised that he would make the perfect detective dog. He had a good nose for spotting things that even I couldn't see, like the old partly-camouflaged tennis ball hidden in the bush or the piece of cake that had fallen off Lara's plate and was half-hidden beneath the sofa. I could also tell that he was a very quick learner because Sam started teaching him new tricks almost as soon as he met him, and Sausage picked them up instantly. The gang thought he was the best dog ever, but none of them developed as close a bond with him as Sam – I could tell straight away that the two of them would be great friends. He was round after school for an hour almost every day teaching him.

And it was looking like a detective dog would certainly come in handy, because we had more and more work on our hands.

On the Wednesday evening after we got Sausage, Lara told me, 'Someone's started trolling me online. She looks like a rival blogger.'

I made her a cup of tea and she told me about somebody with the mysterious initials PLV who had been writing nasty comments on Lara's blog and social media profiles. Most of the messages were short and direct, almost as if PLV were a school bully in the playground. *Get off my patch*, one of them said, while another advised Lara, *If you're doing videos, you should think about getting your hair done. It looks like a bird's nest.*

Lara replied politely, and then when that didn't work, she chose to ignore the messages entirely, but I could tell they were getting under her skin.

'She's claiming I'm stealing other people's recipes and she's telling people to unfollow me because I'm a fraud. Honestly, it's ridiculous.'

'Are you serious?'

'Yeah, and when she saw that photo that you

and Tanya took of me running Cooking Club, she wrote underneath, *Enjoy it while it lasts.* How awful is that?'

'It's terrible,' I agreed. 'What does she mean by that anyway?'

'I really don't know. Do you think I should ask her why she's writing this stuff?'

'But won't that encourage her?'

'I feel I need to say something. Maybe I'll send her a private message. I can't leave it hanging.'

'You can. She's being a horrible troll. If you respond to her, it'll only make it worse. She's a name on a screen. She's writing this stuff because she knows that she can get away with it. She's not saying it to your face, is she?'

'I know, you're right of course. Anyway, you look worried yourself. Is everything OK?'

'Not really. I didn't tell you this before, because you have so much on. But over a week ago now, we found out that Skipton House is being sold.'

Lara's face fell.

'Seriously? Wow, that's big news. Mr Chandler hasn't told me anything.'

'Maybe he hasn't had official confirmation yet. Anyway, hopefully Cooking Club will be moved somewhere else, but I'm thinking about the other stuff that Skipton's used for. Sam was telling me that there's a food bank, and music breakfasts, and day care. Where will all of that go?'

'Surely they'll put together a plan to move it elsewhere. They can't close it all down.'

'Maybe, but what if they don't? And even if they do, it could be far away.'

'Oh love, that's hard. And you're sure this is happening?'

'Yeah, pretty sure. But I've made a plan with Tanya and the boys and Sausage. We're going to somehow find out who the buyer is and persuade them that we need the place more than they do.'

'But how? I don't want to discourage you, because it sounds like a really important cause, but I think it's likely to be a lot more difficult than you think.'

'We're the Cooking Club Detectives,' I told her. 'We're ready for the challenge. I'll keep you posted.'

It was only later, when I was lying in bed

thinking about our next steps in the Skipton Action Plan, that Lara's troll's words came back to me and I realised something important. *Enjoy it while it lasts.* Lara had mentioned Skipton in the post under which PLV had written that. Therefore there was every chance that PLV had something to do with its sale. I was so convinced that I was onto something that I sneaked into the living room and opened Lara's laptop. Sausage was there already and came over, wagging his tail, hoping that I might play with him. I took him onto my lap and stroked him while we looked at the laptop together.

I typed 'PLV' into the search engine. The first thing that came up was 'Powered Light Vehicle' which looked like it was a type of electric car. The next was a scientific article on Partial Liquid Ventilation. I added 'Milwood'.

A cooking blog came up immediately at the top of my search results with the title, *Pasta La Vista*. It couldn't have been more different to Lara's. Its author had chosen a posh, swirly font, it had a logo, which was the shape of a chef's hat made out of a spaghetti strand, and super professional videos to accompany every recipe. They looked as though they'd been made in a recording studio. The branding reminded me of something, and it took me a while to realise that it looked similar to Big Venice – the restaurant sign that I'd spied from the bus on the way to pick up Sausage.

At the top of the page, there was a banner about the opening of a mystery restaurant, but there were very few details. *Everything will be revealed on 1st January*, it said. This was it. It turned out that the mysterious PLV was not quite as mysterious as we'd thought and I had a very good idea about what the location of this new restaurant might be – Skipton.

In the side navigation panel, I found a link to a biography, and when I clicked on it, I saw a familiar face. It was her! The woman with the electric red hair that I'd seen outside Big Venice.

Close up I could see that she was at least ten years older than Lara. She had a white streak in her fringe. The biography below her photo said that her name was Patricia Bell and that she had trained for many years at a well-known chain of fancy restaurants in London. She then became a sous chef in Big Venice.

I was pretty certain that I knew what a sous chef was, but I looked it up again to be sure. Yes – PLV was basically the second in command in the kitchen, below the head chef, and now she was ready to take the final step and run her own show.

I carefully noted down the most important information in my notebook. The biography itself didn't provide any further clues. PLV went on for ages about how she selected only the finest ingredients and liked to focus on the quality of her products. She wrote some bold things, like, *I know pizza and pasta inside out* and *Guaranteed unique and best-tasting recipes on the menu*. There was a link to her Twitter profile, where I managed to find the name of her new venture, in one of her latest tweets.

Step 1 of the big reveal: Vermicelli is the name of my #newrestaurant – I named it after my favourite pasta! More details soon. #pizza #pasta #mostdelicious

I decided that the only way to find out the mystery location would be to go to Big Venice and to somehow get the address.

'We'll go undercover,' I whispered to Sausage. 'I might pretend to be a journalist. I'll say that I came across PLV's blog and wanted to do an interview with her. But maybe she won't believe me because she'll think that I look too young? And anyway, she probably wouldn't give away her secret location for it to be printed in a magazine article. We'll have to keep thinking and be more subtle. Now, you'll have to get a good night's sleep because I'm counting on you to be a super alert detective dog.'

Fifteen

'I have an idea,' said Frixos, when I updated the rest of the Cooking Club Detectives about our new lead over lunch next day. 'We could pretend that we have a delivery for Vermicelli. She must be trying to get it kitted out – we'll go on a day when we know she's not there and we'll ask one of the other members of staff. It's risky, but it's worth a try.'

'But aren't we too young to look like we could be delivering anything?'

'True. But I could ask Gabriel for a favour? He'll do it if he knows that it's for an important mission.'

'OK, if we're going to Arabella's on Saturday, do you think we could fit it in on Sunday?'

'I'll ask him if he's free,' Frixos promised.

'OK, cool. I'll put down those dates in our notebook for now.'

'Frixos, did you manage to find anything out about the property developer?'

'Yes, so they're called Villa Morton and I've got their address and phone number here,' he said, pulling out a crumpled piece of paper from his pocket. 'There was nothing on their website about a new development on Dunstan Row, where Skipton is, but they did say that you can call and enquire well in advance about any new-build flats.'

'I can do it,' said Tanya. 'I'm good at voices. I can make myself sound a lot older. Listen to this.'

She cleared her throat and said in a deep and slightly breathy voice that reminded me of the woman who presents the jazz radio station that Lara likes, 'Hello. This is Cynthia White here. I'm calling to enquire about whether you're planning any new-builds locally. I'm particularly interested in the area around Dunstan Row.'

'Incredible. When can you do it?' asked Sam.

'Whenever. After school today? I can call from my phone and withhold the number.'

'I agree, it's super convincing. I'm wondering if you should mention the specific road? What do you reckon? Do you think it might sound suspicious?'

'Maybe. But Sam, you said they definitely own blocks of flats in the area. They'll probably tell me there are several in Grafton and ask me where in particular I'm looking, so then I can tell them.'

'OK, sounds like a plan,' I said, feeling suddenly hopeful.

We had history after lunch and I couldn't focus on the Wars of the Roses and Henry VII's strategies in battle, even though I loved the Tudors. My hands tingled and part of me was certain that we would get to the bottom of who the buyer was and how to stop them. And then next minute, doubt began to creep in as I imagined the centre being closed and Molly, along with the other parents and carers, being worried about how they would cope without it.

To make things worse, our last lesson of the day was form period with Mr Chandler, who reaffirmed what we already knew.

'I have some news to communicate to members

of Cooking Club. The building in which it's currently held, Skipton House, is in the process of being sold, so it looks like we'll have to find another venue in which to host it. I'm researching at the moment, but if any of you know of anywhere through your families or friends, please let me know.'

'If we ever doubted that it was official, we know for certain now,' said Tanya while we waited for the boys at the front gates after school.

'Yeah, it really is. But at least we've got a plan.'

'Right, we'd better be quick. I can't be too late home,' said Frixos, coming up behind us with Sam. 'Let's go to the netball courts. It's quieter over there. You can put us on loudspeaker and nobody will hear.'

We walked over to the far corner, just to be sure.

Tanya took out her phone, composed herself, and tapped in the number that Sam dictated to her. A male voice picked up on the third ring.

'Villa Morton. How can I help?'

'Oh, hello there. This is Cynthia White. I'm looking for a two-bed property in Grafton – new-build of course – and I wanted to find out what you had available,' said Tanya in her super-convincing voice.

We held our breath, praying that he'd believe she was a real potential buyer.

'Certainly. There's actually quite a lot on offer from us at the moment. Could you give me more detail about what you're after, so that I can narrow down the search?'

'Hmm, I'm pretty open-minded to be honest. I want a place with lots of light, and ideally overlooking some open space if that's possible.'

I crossed my fingers behind my back.

'OK, we have two new projects that might interest you. They're in very early stages. How soon are you looking to move?'

'Oh, it's an investment, you know, I'm happy to wait.'

'In that case I would propose having a look at the brochures for two of our newest locations – one is on Brewer Way and another is off Dunstan Row.'

'Bingo,' mouthed Frixos.

My stomach sank. I'd been hoping beyond hope that it wouldn't be them. A big property development company would be almost impossible to fight.

'Would you like me to email the brochures to you?' the man on the phone continued.

'Erm, actually I've been having some trouble with my email recently,' Tanya improvised with a panicked look on her face. 'But I wondered if I could pick them up from your office tomorrow. Or perhaps my son could, if I'm busy.'

I was certain at that point that the man had seen through us and that we were busted, but to my surprise, he said, 'Absolutely. I'll leave them in an envelope for you in reception. We're open from eight a.m. to six p.m. Can I take your name again? And your phone number for our records.'

Tanya repeated her fake name, dictated a number that I was certain wasn't hers, and said goodbye.

We sat in silence for a couple of seconds after she hung up.

'It's them,' I said.

'We don't know for certain,' said Sam.

'It is. Come on, Sam, you heard it yourself. A development just off Dunstan Row. It must be.

They're much more obvious than Ali's aunt or PLV. How are we ever going to fight them?' I asked. I suddenly felt a tell-tale prickling in the corner of my eyes.

'I'll go there before school tomorrow,' said Frixos. 'Their office is on the high street, right? I'll say I'm Cynthia's son and then we can go from there.'

Sixteen

'So lovely to see you,' was the first thing Lara said when I got home. She was sitting at the kitchen table still dressed in her pyjama bottoms and a baggy T-shirt, which was unlike her.

'You too,' I said. 'What's been going on?'

'I've been battling the trolls again. I reached an exciting milestone this morning of five thousand followers on Instagram, and I've had almost eight thousand readers on the blog since it started, so I wrote a post to say thank you and that I hoped people found my recipes useful. I had loads of lovely comments, but then PLV popped up out of nowhere saying that my recipes are simple and unoriginal and that cheap ingredients mean that my meals aren't nutritious. She wrote under a different account name, but I could tell straight away that it was her from the style of her writing.'

'Yeah,' I said, hanging up my rucksack and coat, 'she loves banging on about using the best ingredients.'

'How do you know?' asked Lara, smiling. 'Have you been spying on her?'

'Yeah,' I said, feeling my cheeks burning, 'I was intrigued.'

'Anyway, she's not even the biggest of my worries. There are a couple of other people who are now accusing me of taking money for advertising. They're saying that I'm promoting myself as a person who does low-cost recipes, while I secretly make millions through advertising. "Millions" is what somebody actually wrote. I don't know what planet they're living on. We'd be living in a beach house on an island in the middle of the Pacific Ocean if I was actually making millions.'

'Oh, that's awful.' I went to give her a hug. 'You know they're only writing that stuff because they're jealous and it's easy for them to do it from the safety of their laptops.'

'You're right, but I got into a stupid conversation trying to explain my position and I realise now that I shouldn't have because it only made the whole thing worse.'

'Don't worry about that now,' I said. 'Ignore the online bullies next time.'

'I know, I will.'

We spent a cosy evening curled up on the sofa with Sausage, watching *The Lion King*. It's such a cool film, it cheered her up and took my mind off worries about the property development company. I was so relaxed I managed to fall asleep in front of the TV.

I dreamed about standing with Sam, Tanya and Frixos in front of a huge oak desk, behind which a bald man with round glasses was sitting. He was typing away furiously on his computer, and there were several phones around him which kept ringing. He answered them angrily, each time refusing to do what the person on the other end of the line wanted.

'I keep telling you – "no" – the decision has already been made. Which part of that isn't clear to you?' he barked.

I was conscious of the others pushing me to the front of the queue, trying to hide behind me.

'Ask him,' they said. 'You have to ask him. Otherwise, we'll never know.'

But I opened my mouth to tell him about Cooking Club and to beg that he withdraw his offer for Skipton House, only to find that my voice had completely gone.

'It's not Skipton,' shouted Frixos from down the hallway when he came to find us the following morning at breaktime.

'Shhh... Stop being so loud,' hissed Tanya, dragging him to a quiet spot next to the library. 'What's not Skipton?'

'I got the brochures this morning,' he said, passing them to us, 'and the development on Dunstan Row is much further along than Skipton. It's at the far end of the road. You know, almost on the edge of the woods.'

He turned over one of the brochures and showed

us a map on which a red cross marked where the development would be. He was right. It wasn't even anywhere close.

'So, Sam was right, it's *not* them,' I said in disbelief. I felt like an invisible enemy had been pressing a knee to my chest and had suddenly let go. One lead down – but we still had two more to investigate; our detective work was definitely not over. The weekend plan was still on.

'It's not. I even asked at reception if this was the only development planned on that road, and they said it was,' said Frixos proudly.

'Great detective work,' said Tanya, giving him a high five. 'So the search continues, and tomorrow we'll go to Arabella's. We need to be subtle though. We can't ask her where her new place is, because she might not want to tell us. I was thinking that we could say that someone we know is planning an event in the future. We can even say it's like a big party that's a year away and that the guests are coming from all over the country, or even abroad, and will need somewhere to stay. Then we can get someone on reception to talk us through the different properties.'

'Great plan. You're good at this,' I said to her, admiringly.

'Thanks. Bring Sausage though. He's our detective dog and if he distracts them, they'll be far more likely to give us some answers.'

'It's really annoying that I can't come. I really want to,' said Frixos. 'Especially if Sausage is going too.'

'I know, but you're coming on Sunday, right? Remember, we're going to Big Venice.' I'd told them everything that I'd managed to find out about Pasta La Vista and we'd finalised our plan of action with Gabriel acting as our pretend supplier.

'Of course, we're on.'

Seventeen

The following morning, I couldn't wait to get out of the house. I had the perfect idea for what we would tell Arabella – it wouldn't even be a lie, because it was something that I'd been planning in my head for a long time – Lara's thirty-fifth birthday. We'd never properly celebrated her thirtieth, because I'd been too young to organise anything, so we'd decided that her thirty-fifth would be a big one. It was still months away, but I knew that she'd want a proper party, with excellent food of course, and all the people she loved. I was hoping that Aunty Sarah and her family would come over from Australia. I'd already had a few ideas about where to host the event, but that was before we'd moved house, so now I would have to start looking again.

Wherever it was, there would definitely be guests who would be coming from different parts of the UK, and Lara's best friend lives in the South of France – they would need a place to stay.

'I'm off,' I shouted to Lara, who was having a lie-in. The day before I'd told her that I wanted to hang out with Tanya in the morning and that I would take Sausage. It was good timing, because she was planning to meet up with a friend for lunch in the high street.

'Have a good day, love!' she shouted back. I imagined her diving under the covers for another doze.

Sam met me at the corner of the street and together we headed to Tanya's.

She opened the door almost the second I took my finger off the bell. 'Come in,' she said, edging backwards as Sausage tried to jump on her. 'I thought I'd make us a quick breakfast.'

She was wearing a floral apron and as soon as we walked into the kitchen, she resumed what she must have been doing earlier, which involved pouring something into a sizzling pan.

'I'm trying to master Mrs Gupta's pancakes,' she said. 'I need to start somewhere and her recipe looked relatively easy, so… here goes!'

I went over to get a closer look at the mixture. It seemed as though she'd got the quantities right, and it was just the technique which wasn't quite there. The first pancake that she produced was slightly undercooked and too thick.

'Help me out, guys,' she said. 'What's going wrong here?'

'Pour less of the mixture in,' I told her.

'And shall I help you flip?' asked Sam. 'I've become a pro.'

For her first ever batch at home, it was a pretty good effort, and I think neither Sam nor I had realised how hungry we were. Sausage was also rubbing his nose against my leg, which was a sure sign that he was ravenous. I got him a bowl of water and gave him a few chewy treats from my bag.

As we ate, I noticed a photo pinned to the notice board above our heads in which a young-looking man with short dreadlocks was lifting Jayden above his head. The two of them were in fits of laughter, as if the photographer had caught them mid-joke. Both were wearing the same football shirt.

'Who's that?' I asked.

'Oh, that's Dad,' said Tanya. 'I forgot that you haven't met him yet.'

I was surprised – I'd always imagined Tanya's dad as a businessman in an immaculate suit, but the man in the photo looked so relaxed and kind.

'It was taken at Jayden's last birthday party. He was having a tough time because this boy in school was bullying him and it really affected Jayden's self-esteem. He started thinking that nobody liked him and that people wouldn't turn up to his party. So Dad organised a surprise party for him and loads of kids ended up coming. He also spent ages chatting to him about why he's special and important – he's always really great with him.'

'I'm glad he had a good time,' said Sam. 'Why do people have to be bullies?'

'Who knows? It was tough for Jayden at first, but things are better now and he's enjoying school. Anyway, we'd better get going,' said Tanya, noticing that we'd finished eating. 'We want to get to Arabella's in good time.'

It took us much longer to get to the B&B than I'd expected. The number fifteen bus made so many stops on the way that I thought we'd never get there, and then we had to walk, which involved Sausage stopping at every tree to give it a good sniff. Sam, who was holding his lead, refused to tug on it to make him go faster.

'Let him explore,' he said fondly.

When we finally arrived, I was surprised by the building in front of me. I didn't have an exact vision in my mind, but knowing Ali, I'd expected it to be glamorous. Instead, I saw a cottage on a quiet lane with ivy climbing the wall and rose bushes at the front door. *Your home away from home*, said a sign hanging in one of the windows.

'This is it,' said Tanya. 'Let's go in. You do the talking, yeah?'

We bundled into the reception area filled with old, floral armchairs and little glass side-tables.

'Can I help?' asked a bored-looking young man. He must have been around the same age as Gabriel.

'Yeah, I wondered if the owner's here?' I asked, realizing how nervous I sounded.

'She won't be in for another hour. Why do you need her?' he asked suspiciously.

At that point I clammed up and Tanya had to rescue me.

'Look, Arabella is my friend's aunt. And Erin here was thinking of booking this place – and maybe even the other B&Bs too, because she's planning a surprise party for her mum's birthday.'

'Right,' said the boy, still looking bored. The fact that Tanya knew the owner seemed to have made no impression on him whatsoever. 'So why didn't you call or send an email?'

'We were passing through,' I said, 'and I've never been here before, so I thought I might get a chance to check it out in real life.'

'You'll have to come back when she's here,' he said.

At this point, Sausage gave a low growl, which I'd never heard him do before. It was so unexpected from such a good-natured dog, and even the boy stepped back, unsure of what to do.

'Come on, let's go,' I said to Sausage, pulling him gently by the lead, but my dog wouldn't budge.

'It looks like we'll have to wait,' said Sam calmly, making himself comfortable in one of the armchairs.

The boy took a phone out of his pocket, turned his back on us and made a call. A minute or so later, a lady appeared through the double doors to our right. She was wearing a green dress with a floral collar that matched the armchairs, and a frilled apron that looked as if it came from the Victorian times.

'So what can I help you with, Derek?' she asked impatiently.

'I wondered if you could, erm, see these people in Arabella's absence.'

'Right, is it not something you can deal with yourself?'

Her entire face suddenly changed when she saw Sausage.

'Oh my goodness, what a beautiful dog. You know he looks so much like my Charlie? He passed away last year sadly but he lived to a grand old age. His father was a Labrador. What's this little fella called?'

'This is Sausage,' I said, and then the rest of us introduced ourselves.

'I'm Margaret,' she replied, smiling at us. She put her hands out and Sausage sniffed them. He clearly seemed to think a lot more of her than he did of Derek and I began to think my dog was in fact a very good judge of character.

'Does he know any tricks?'

'Yes, I've been training him,' said Sam proudly. 'I'll show you. But maybe we should go outside, because there's not much space in here.'

'Good idea, I've got five minutes to spare so you can let me know how I can help you. There's a field to the right of our back garden, which will be perfect. Let's go. It's windy, but still pretty warm for October. I can't believe it's almost Halloween.'

I could hear Derek breathe a sigh of relief as we left.

Sausage was in his element, and Margaret made a huge fuss of him. Sam proudly showed off how my dog had already learned to give you his paw on demand and how he could beg for a treat, but Sausage wouldn't focus nearly as well as he did at our flat. There were too many things that excited and distracted him. He spent ages chasing a fly he spotted in the grass and we had to put his lead back on, as we were worried he'd run off into the road.

'Oh, he's a beauty,' Margaret said, when we finally sat down in the field to catch our breath. 'He's made me realise how much I miss Charlie. He was my constant companion, you know. Bella used to let me bring him to work as long as he stayed in the garden, or our staffroom, so I could spend most of my days with him.'

'Bella as in Arabella?' asked Tanya. 'Have you worked with her for long?'

'Yes – Arabella. Would you believe we went to school together? It feels like a lifetime ago now – almost forty years. We had our own lives back then and had completely different jobs, but she contacted me as soon as she was looking into starting her B&B business and asked if I wanted to be part of it. We've been running for ten years now and it's not going too badly. She does the bookings and the management side of things, and I look after the suppliers and the catering. I still oversee the breakfasts here. It gets me up in the mornings and I enjoy that part of the day. Did you say you knew Bella?'

'She's my friend's aunt,' said Tanya. 'We came today to find out about making a reservation for next year. Erin is planning a big party for her mum next summer and needs somewhere for her guests to stay. How many people can you sleep in total?'

'Well, let me see. We have six double bedrooms here. But the other two places are bigger. They're within ten minutes of the town centre. What's your venue for the party?'

'Oh, I haven't actually decided on one yet, but I have a few front runners,' I improvised. 'They're central, so I'm sure your other two places will be fine.'

'Sure, well the one on Nightingale Road is ten doubles, and the same goes for Gibney Road.'

'And you've only got the three? You're not planning on opening any more next year if business goes well?'

Tanya asked in such a light, joking tone, that there was no way that Margaret could suspect anything, but I still found myself holding my breath.

'Not yet. We debated it about six months ago, but then there was a pretty major leak at Nightingale Road and we realised that most of the roof would need replacing. So a lot of money went into that. It's a shame as we had our eye on this lovely Victorian place at the end of the high street near the old mill. It's been sold now. But everything happens for a reason and it's made us wonder whether we should look further afield.'

'Oh I'm sure you'll find the perfect place when the time is right,' smiled Tanya smoothly. 'Anyway, Margaret, you've given us loads of useful info about the rooms you have. So Erin, when you've set the date of the party, I reckon we'll give Arabella a call, right?'

'Yes,' I said, nodding. But my brain was already in overdrive. Our first two leads had been eliminated. That left PLV, Pasta La Vista. Surely, it had to be her. I'd done some further research online to check whether she'd posted about her restaurant opening. There wasn't anything on her social media, but then I came across a short interview in a cooking magazine, in which she revealed that the restaurant would be in a *pleasant, leafy, out of town setting* – a description which exactly fitted Skipton.

On our way back to Tanya's we plotted our strategy for the following day. Sam was going to ring Frixos to remind him about asking Gabriel to help us and we would meet at the bus stop opposite the post office on the high street at ten a.m. The number fifteen would drop us round the corner from Pasta La Vista's restaurant.

'I'm certain that it's her, you know,' I told Sam on the way home. 'How are we going to persuade her not to buy Skipton?'

'I think it's always best to be honest,' said Sam thoughtfully. 'We'll have to show her that we need it more than she does.'

Eighteen

Sam's words were still running through my mind the following morning as I walked with him and Sausage to the bus stop. We'd been so focused on finding the real buyer that we hadn't considered what we would do when we actually found them. Even if we were honest, it struck me that convincing them to change their minds would be nearly impossible.

At the start of our investigation, I'd imagined that Pasta La Vista would be the easiest buyer to deal with. She wasn't part of a huge company like Villa Morton, and she wasn't looking to acquire more properties, like Arabella. But the more I'd watched her videos and read her blog, the more I understood how ambitious she was.

From her online personality, it was obvious that she would put up a dirty fight.

I had everything crossed that Gabriel would be there with Frixos, because who would believe a group of kids saying that they had something to deliver to a restaurant?

Luckily, he was there, waiting for us at the bus stop with Frixos and Tanya.

'He can't stay long,' Frixos said straight away.

'Yeah, sorry – I promised I'd meet some mates to discuss a website that we've been working on.'

'Don't worry. We'll be quick. Has Frixos told you the plan?'

'Sort of. I'm supposed to be saying that I'm delivering some stuff to a new restaurant that this woman is opening.'

'Exactly. Do you remember her name?' asked Frixos, testing his brother.

'Patricia Bell.'

'Excellent.'

'And what's her restaurant called?'

'Cannelloni?'

'Wrong! Vermicelli.'

'I was only messing,' Gabriel said, winking at Frixos.

The bus arrived and we piled on.

'But what am I supposed to say? I didn't bring any props.'

'Argh, we didn't think about that, did we?' Tanya panicked.

'No, don't worry.' I had this one covered. 'You just say that your van is parked down the street, because you couldn't find a closer parking spot. Remember, the main thing is to get the address of the new restaurant. So you need to find someone who looks like a junior member of staff and say something like, "Hi, I've got a delivery for Vermicelli, Patricia Bell's new place. I wondered if you could give me directions, I know it's not far from here." Hopefully they'll tell you with no fuss.'

'OK, sure. That sounds easy enough. And if they ask questions?'

'What sort of questions?'

'Like about what I'm delivering? Or what company I work for?'

'Good point. Say something like "kitchen equipment". Let's think of a company name.'

'Restaurant Solutions?' suggested Sam.

'Yes, that could work. What's this all about anyway?'

'Can't tell you,' said Frixos, 'top secret. Only members of the Cooking Club Detectives can know for now.'

'Right, OK…'

The journey didn't take long and most of my time was spent chasing Sausage around the bus. He insisted on sniffing every fellow passenger and trying to do his best to look through the back window. I was relieved when we were finally able to get off.

'Do you want to take Sausage with you?' I asked Gabriel. 'He's our official detective dog and he provides a great distraction. We've already put him to work on our last suspect.'

'Er, sure. I can give it a try.'

The blue restaurant looked the same as when I'd seen it on the bus with Lara, and I half expected PLV's red head to appear through the doorway.

'We'll wait here. You go ahead,' I said to Gabriel.

'It looks pretty quiet,' he said. 'I can't see any clients in there.'

'That's because they've probably only just started to prepare lunch. The customers haven't arrived yet. It's the perfect time. Go!'

We watched him walk down the road, Sausage barking excitedly by his side.

'We'll know that it's her for certain any minute now,' I said. I was feeling confident and, at the same time, worried about what was coming.

'Or not,' said Frixos. 'You never know. We might have to cast the net wider with our suspects.'

We sat on a bench across the street, trying to look casual. From my position, I could make out Gabriel through the glass. He was chatting to a young waitress with a long, blonde ponytail. I could see her patting Sausage's head – the conversation looked like it was going well. Then she suddenly disappeared somewhere and he was left waiting. The minutes stretched into infinity. Eventually she came back with what looked like an older man holding a clipboard.

This is it, I thought. I'd forgotten to tell Gabriel to write down the address on his phone. I hoped his memory would be good enough.

'Why do you think it's taking so long?'

'Maybe they're telling him more about the new restaurant,' whispered Tanya.

Finally, Gabriel appeared in the doorway. He took a minute to spot us, and when he did, he broke into a half-run.

'They're not happy,' he said, when he and Sausage reached us, both panting. 'In fact, they're suspicious. They even asked whether I'd been sent by a newspaper. Anyway, they wouldn't reveal the address and they told me to email her if I couldn't get through on the phone. So I've got the email address for you, but nothing else.'

'Oh no! That totally backfired. I'm sorry!' I felt awful for having put him through that. Clearly I'd underestimated PLV's levels of suspicion.

'Did you give your real name or anything?' asked Frixos, looking scared.

'No, no, don't worry. I said I was called Dennis Dunkers. It was the first thing that came into my head. I'm not sure they believed me, but it doesn't matter. Anyway, I've got to run. I'm already late. Good luck with whatever it is you're doing!'

'Thanks, Gabriel,' I said. 'We appreciate it.'

As soon as he left, Frixos asked, 'But what are we going to do now? It sounds like she doesn't trust anyone.'

'We could try and break into her office and have a rummage around for the address?' Frixos suggested.

'How do you know that she even has an office? Isn't she always cooking?'

'So what then? Break into her house?' Frixos continued.

'No. I don't think we should do any breaking in,' Tanya protested. 'That could end badly.'

'Why don't we send her an email and pretend it's from the current owner of Skipton? Then if it really is the place she's buying, she'll reply and if not, she'll write something back to say that we've emailed the wrong person.'

'There's also the chance that she won't reply,' said Sam. 'Because if it is her, she'd already be communicating with the owner and she'll realise that you're not him.'

'Exactly. I reckon we need to speak to her in person. Let me think about this some more.'

We headed back on the number fifteen. Sam went to check that his grandma didn't need anything, and Frixos waved us goodbye, but Tanya wasn't in a rush to go home. She pulled nervously at one of her braids.

'Are you all right?' I asked her. 'You look worried about something.'

'What? No, no. I'm trying to think what to do next about Pasta La Vista,' she said. 'Gosh, she seems awful, doesn't she?'

'Yeah. She's been horrible to my mum. But this restaurant thing clearly means a lot to her which is why she's keeping it such a secret.'

'If I tell you something, do you promise not to get mad at me?'

'Depends what it is,' I said, but then when I saw how anxious she looked I told her I was joking. 'I promise. Go on.'

'Well, I looked her up myself, because I was

curious, and I have to admit that I sort of... liked her blog. Obviously it's nowhere near as good as Lara's, but she does have some decent recipes. And – please don't be angry – I tried one of them because the picture looked so delicious. It was a fig and orange salad and Ana had just bought some figs and anyway... I'm not sure why I'm telling you this really. I suppose I wanted to get it off my chest, because I know she's not a nice person...'

A bubble of hilarity rose slowly in my throat and before I could stop myself, I was laughing so hard my stomach hurt.

'What?' asked Tanya, shocked.

'I don't hate you,' I said, trying to get my breath back. 'Is that why you've been acting weird? It's good that you did some proper research into her, even if it's an unusual way to go about it.'

We'd almost reached the door to my flat when something occurred to me. 'Hey, I've had a brilliant idea. Why don't you send her an email and say that you're a fan and ask whether you could meet her? You could even tell her that you made a salad according to her recipe? Maybe you could say that you and your friend – me – would love to get her autograph. She probably won't respond, but in the meantime we can keep thinking about other ways to find out if she's our suspect.'

Tanya considered the idea. I could see her weighing up the risks in her head.

'Sure, let's do it. Only I'm not *really* a fan. You know that, right? I still think that your mum is the best chef ever. I'm doing this to save Cooking Club so that she can continue teaching us.'

'I know, I know. Don't worry,' I said, and the two of us tried to bundle Sausage into the flat. It was becoming quite a mission, as he was loving the outdoors so much that he never wanted to come inside.

Lara wasn't back yet, so we gave Sausage an early dinner and sat down together in my room to try to write the perfect email to PLV, one which would make her want to meet us. This is what we came up with:

Dear Patricia,

My name is Tanya, I'm in Year Seven and I've been reading your blog for some time now. I'm a big fan of your recipes. You create so many delicious-looking dishes. Yesterday, I made your fig and orange salad and it was out of this world. Even my dad loved it, and he doesn't really like oranges.

Anyway, the answer will probably be no, but I wondered if there was any chance that I could meet you? I would love to get an autograph, and maybe you could even show me how you make one of your dishes? It would be great to see you at work in real life.

All the best,

Tanya Anukem

'Perhaps it won't come to anything, but it's worth a try. I'm starving,' said Tanya.

I brought out Lara's recipe book, which was really my recipe book now, and together we chose to make veggie burgers, mainly because we happened to have the ingredients we needed.

'This is incredible,' said Tanya, admiring the battered notebook.

It only took us half an hour to make the veggie

burgers, which were delicious and warming – exactly what we needed.

Victorious Veggie Burgers

Ingredients

- 1 tin pinto or black beans (other varieties also work)
- 3 tablespoons tomato puree
- Half a teaspoon salt
- 2 tablespoons flour, self-raising or plain
- 2 cooked, diced carrots
- 4 burger buns
- 4 slices of cheddar cheese
- 1 tomato, sliced

Method

1. First, drain and rinse the beans, then mash them with a fork or in a food processor.

2. Add the tomato puree, salt, flour and diced carrots and mix together well. Then form into patties. There should be enough to make four in total.

3. Place the patties on a parchment-lined baking tray and bake at 180°C for 10 minutes, then flip and bake for another 10 minutes.

4. When ready, serve inside the buns with a slice of tomato and cheese. Enjoy!

'They were yum,' said Tanya, 'but now I should be heading home.'

Before she did, I asked her to check her email on the off-chance that something had come in – and there it was. To our disbelief, a message from Patricia Bell was nestling in her inbox. She read it out loud.

Dear Tanya,

Thank you for writing to me. It's so nice to hear from a fan! I would love to meet you and give you a little goody bag, and my autograph, if you like. I'm quite busy at the moment, so won't have time for a cooking session.

Would you like to come with a friend and an adult to my restaurant? Weekends are busy for me, but maybe a Monday, Wednesday or Thursday after school at around 4.30 p.m?

Best wishes,

Patricia

'No way! She totally wants to meet you! We need to go as soon as possible. Let's reply and ask her if she's free tomorrow. If she is, we can maybe ask your dad if he can come with us? We can't ask my mum because they might recognise each other and anyway PLV is the enemy.'

'Sounds good. I doubt that my dad will have time, but I'll ask Ana. If she doesn't need to take Jayden anywhere, she'll be able to come with us.'

'All right, it's a plan. My mum would be so disappointed in us if she found out we were talking to the enemy.'

'She wouldn't if you explained why we're doing

it,' said Tanya. 'Hey, don't you think that PLV sounds surprisingly nice in her email?'

'Well, of course she's nice to you – you've praised her blog and said how much you love her recipes.'

'True. I'm intrigued to see what she's like in person.'

'We'll find out soon enough.'

Nineteen

'Ana's agreed,' said Tanya, the minute we sat down in form period next day. 'We can go after school. I've emailed PLV back. You know, the more I've thought about it, the more I'm certain that it's her. The problem is that I don't know whether she'll tell us the truth.'

Mr Chandler went through a list of notices to start the week off and gave us an update on Cooking Club.

'I'm still waiting for official confirmation, but we should have a place sorted for Cooking Club, so that we can continue running it. Unfortunately, it looks like the community centre hasn't yet found a new venue, which means that we will have to go solo on this and rent our own space. There's a room in the town hall which is available on Thursday evenings, but we might have to ask parents to help us cover the costs of the rental. I'll give you letters to take home once we have everything finalised.'

I immediately thought of Sam's grandma and lots of other parents and carers who probably wouldn't have the money for this.

At lunchtime, we filled the boys in on our email to Pasta La Vista (omitting the bit about Tanya actually liking her recipes in real life).

'But what will you say when you finally meet her?' Frixos asked, raising an eyebrow.

'That's what we haven't planned yet,' I admitted.

'Make sure you take Sausage. Even she might soften when she sees a nice dog. Maybe keep it gentle and say that you heard about her new restaurant opening and sort of try to get a sense of the location by asking her if it's nearby.'

'I actually think that you should be bold and upfront,' Sam argued. 'If she asks you anything about whether you like cooking, say that you do and that you've been going to Cooking Club at the local community centre in Skipton House. Ask her if she knows it and see if she flinches. You'll be able to tell straight away from her expression.'

'I agree,' said Tanya. 'It's about watching the way that she behaves. I'm a good judge of people's expressions. I'll be able to tell if she's lying.'

'We can definitely try. Let's see how the conversation goes and we'll sort of improvise.'

And that's exactly what we did.

We sped home to get Sausage, telling Lara that we were taking him for a walk. I felt so guilty about lying to her that I couldn't even look her in the eye. Then we hurried to Tanya's house to pick up Ana, who was already waiting for us, dressed in a flowing dress and a nice yellow coat.

'I rarely have a chance to wear something fancy, so I thought I would today,' she said, winking at me as I admired her outfit.

We decided to walk to the restaurant as it was only about fifteen minutes away. Ana made a huge fuss of Sausage and asked if she could hold his lead.

'Are you such a big fan of this lady too?' she asked me.

'Not as much as Tanya, but I'd still like to meet her,' I said, as honestly as I could.

'Well, it's nice to get an insight into the sorts of things that you're into, Tanya. I didn't realise that you were so interested in cooking these days, until you made that pizza. I have to say that was one of the best pizzas I've had in a long time. I think we should reverse our roles in the kitchen and maybe I can learn something from you now!'

'You used my mum's pizza recipe?' I asked her, and she nodded proudly.

'It was delicious. I was surprised. I thought I would mess it up.'

We started telling Ana about the other dishes we'd made in Cooking Club, and I relaxed so much that I almost forgot where we were heading. It was only when we were round the corner from Big Venice, that the nerves kicked in. I had a vision of us being rejected as Gabriel had been, which was silly, of course, because we'd been invited especially.

We walked through the double doors and were

greeted by a smiling waitress – possibly the same one Gabriel had spoken to. Sausage sniffed around with interest. I wondered whether we'd be able to tell anything from his first reaction to PLV. Would he growl at her too?

'Hello, we're here to see Patricia. She invited us to come and meet her.'

'Let me go and see if she's available.'

And a few minutes later Patricia herself emerged with her shock of red hair and the stark white stripe in her fringe. She was wearing her chef's uniform, which was a brilliant, clean white with the bright red logo on the left breast.

'How lovely to see you,' she said, beaming, but I couldn't help but be on guard. 'Which one of you is Tanya?'

'That's me,' said Tanya nervously. 'And this is Ana and my friend Erin and her dog Sausage. Thanks so much for inviting us to see you.'

'No, no, the pleasure is mine,' said Patricia. I noticed that her expression changed when she saw Sausage – it was as though even her eyes were smiling.

Sausage wriggled away behind my legs, but otherwise seemed quite calm. I noted this with interest – he clearly didn't think that she was all bad news. Even though she seemed nice, I couldn't forget the nasty comments she had made about Lara's recipes.

'I'm afraid we can't allow dogs into the restaurant,' she said, looking genuinely sad, 'but he can wait here for us and I'll bring him a treat. What does he like eating? I have some tasty chicken that he might like.'

'Yeah,' I said, surprised. 'I think he would be up for that.'

She disappeared behind a black door and was back moments later carrying two bowls. 'I thought I'd give him some water too, in case he's thirsty. Come here, lovely boy.' She placed them both in front of Sausage and tickled him gently behind the ear.

'Let me show you around, shall I? And then I'll give you a goody bag to go home with. Let's start in the kitchen.'

Patricia took us through the black swing door

behind which a massive kitchen stretched out. The smells were divine. On one side there was a huge clay oven into which a chef was placing a pizza on a shovel. On the other, a couple of kitchen assistants were chopping vegetables, and another was cleaning and filleting a fish.

'This still isn't properly clean, Martin,' she barked at him, running her finger across one of the surfaces as we walked by. I noticed that it was gleaming.

'Sorry, chef! I'll do it again, chef!' he answered. It almost sounded like they were in the army.

'So this is where the magic happens,' said PLV. 'We normally serve around fifty guests on an average evening, and obviously more at weekends. We specialise in Italian cuisine, and we're particularly focused on fish dishes with a difference, making them unique to our menu.'

'And you're also going to be doing Italian food at your new place, right?' said Tanya, sounding enthusiastic.

'Yes, exactly. That's been my area of expertise for many years. It's opening soon now which I'm ecstatic about. Anyway, come through.'

She showed us the two main dining spaces, which had elaborate gold paintings on the walls. One was of fire and the other of water.

'We separate our menu into two distinct food groups, depending on tastes. We call one of them "Fire" – for the more spicy palate – and the other "Water" – for the calmer flavours.'

'Can I take a look?' asked Ana. 'I've never been here before. I'm curious.'

'Of course.' PLV handed each of us two menus – one had fiery pizzas and pastas, full of chilli flakes and paprika, and the other was filled with creamy broths and comforting tomatoey tastes. It was then I saw the prices. There were pizzas on the menu for £17 and a king prawn pasta dish that cost £28.

'Expensive.' The word came out before I realised that I'd said it aloud.

'Yes. I like to focus on the highest quality fresh ingredients, and I'm afraid that comes at a price.'

I could feel the blood rushing to my cheeks.

'It doesn't have to,' I said. 'Some good, fresh food can be bought cheaply at the supermarket. It's all about knowing where and how to shop for food.'

'That may be true, although I doubt it's the case for many items. But our clients have refined palates, and they're also paying for a night off from cooking. They want to soak up the atmosphere and enjoy a delicious meal.' The way that she said it annoyed me – as though it was something obvious that everyone could understand.

'But what about the people who can't afford posh restaurants and also want to enjoy a decent meal?'

PLV seemed so taken aback that she stopped in her tracks. By that point I'd realised suddenly that I didn't care about her opinion.

'That's why it's really sad that you're opening a restaurant in a place that so many people love and use, to cook for those who have loads of money anyway and can afford to eat anywhere,' I babbled.

I could feel the tears pricking my eyelids.

'What's wrong, Erin?' asked Ana gently. 'What's brought this on?'

The four of us sat at one of the tables. I was angry at myself for struggling to control my voice.

'It's about Skipton House – our community centre. It's where we have Cooking Club and where they put on a breakfast for kids who otherwise might not always get it. They run judo and music, and dance clubs, and loads of other great services. It brings together people who might otherwise never be friends. I'm going to miss it immensely when it goes. I think Tanya will too, but at least we're lucky in that we don't *need* it. But there are other families who rely on it, and I know that they're worried about what they'll do when it goes.'

'OK...' said PLV carefully, looking confused. 'But why are they closing it down if it's so useful to so many people? Did you want me to do something to help you keep it open? Write a letter?'

I looked at her, dumbstruck.

'I... I don't want you to open your restaurant there,' I blurted out, although even as I said it, I knew what was coming.

'Sorry? My restaurant? You think I'm opening it at the same location as your community centre?'

'Yes. Skipton House on Dunstan Row. Aren't you?'

'No. I can tell you for certain that I'm not. Whatever led you to think that I was?'

'It's just that…' I stopped, deciding that it would be a very bad idea to mention Lara now. 'Well, we were following your blog and you were being so secretive about the location of your new place and in one of the interviews that you did, the description of where it was fitted our community centre exactly.'

'But it could fit a lot of places,' said PLV, slightly impatient now. 'I was being deliberately vague so that it couldn't be pinned down to a particular place. You might think I'm an idiot keeping it a secret, but the truth is that I've worked so hard for so many years. I started washing pans and chopping vegetables, and being told off for the smallest mistakes, and eventually I picked up new skills in the kitchen, and decided that I wanted to specialise in pizza and pasta, and my dishes were finally being recognised and… What I mean is,' she concluded, trying to stay calm, 'is that this opening is my greatest achievement, and I want to make the most of it by keeping it a surprise for everyone until the very end.'

'But it's definitely not Skipton House?' Tanya checked for the final time.

'No. It's not. It's on a completely different road, in a building that's been empty for a few years now. That's all I can tell you. And here I was thinking that you wrote to me because you genuinely liked my food.'

'I do,' Tanya protested. 'What I wrote in the email wasn't a lie.'

'I'm sorry,' I mumbled. My hands were shaking, and I felt exhausted – as if I'd reached the end of a very long race, in which I'd come last.

'Well,' said PLV, sighing. 'You clearly feel strongly about this place – I admire that. Maybe you should start a petition to try to keep it open? Gather the signatures of everyone who loves it and benefits from it. They often work.'

'I could,' I admitted, 'I hadn't thought of that.'

'It's a good idea,' said Tanya, but I could see that she was as disappointed as I was.

'Seeing as you're here, let me at least give you your goody bags,' said Pasta La Vista.

As the first customers started to arrive for dinner, we took it as our cue to leave.

'Thank you for inviting us,' said Ana beaming.

'It's been a pleasure.'

Tanya and I shook Pasta La Vista's hand, firmly this time, before we walked out with Sausage into the cool evening air.

'Back to the beginning of the search,' I said, sighing.

'We'll get there,' said Tanya, squeezing my hand.

Twenty

I couldn't sleep that night, as different visions of who the Skipton purchaser might be ran through my mind. Was it another huge property developer? A supermarket? A shopping centre? Another school? The more I thought about it, the more the possibilities seemed endless.

At breakfast, Lara did her best to console me. At first, I didn't want to tell her that we'd gone to see PLV behind her back, but she could see how upset I was and in the end, I couldn't hide it from her. I told her the full story.

'Pasta La Vista? Oh Erin, that's not PLV,' said Lara. 'I know Pasta La Vista – not personally I mean, I know *of* her. I even looked at her blog for some inspiration when I was first writing mine. She has a huge following on social media and she's very well respected. She wouldn't write comments like that.'

'What? It's *not* her? Who is it then?'

'Well, one of my followers, Clarissa, who's becoming a fairly well-known shoe designer, recently got in touch with me to say that PLV has also been writing nasty comments on *her* posts. Later, a reputation agency called "Verified Likes and Praise" got in touch with her and said that they would deal with any online bullies and help build up her followers and likes. And guess what?'

'They got in touch with you too.'

'Yeah – only a couple of days later. It's a scam. A very expensive one too. They posed as a troll and posted negative comments on my site, then asked for a heap of money every month to help me manage my reputation.'

'PLV – it's their initials reversed.'

'Hey, I didn't even notice that. You really do have a nose for detective work. I've reported PLV's account now and blocked it.'

'Good work.'

'But Pasta La Vista – she really might have a point about the petition you know. They do often work.'

'Do you honestly think so?'

'It's definitely worth a try. The main thing is not to give up hope.'

At breaktime Tanya and I told the boys about our visit to Pasta La Vista's and I revealed what Lara had told me about PLV and how it had turned out to be a false lead.

'No way. What an awful scam,' said Frixos. 'I bet some people fall for it if they're really desperate.'

'Never mind that. We're back where we started,' I said. 'I think our only hope now is to start a petition. Edgar hasn't replied to us, so we'll have to go and meet him in person. And our argument will be much stronger if we have the backing of loads of people.'

'Let's do it tonight,' said Tanya. 'Do you want to come to mine after school?'

Neither of the boys were free, but I agreed to help and we planned to distribute the petition the next day.

So that evening, we took Tanya's laptop to the kitchen and searched for 'sample petitions'. A range of fancy templates appeared, as well as portals that allowed you to set up a petition online and send a link, asking people to sign it. They looked quite technical and complicated and I couldn't imagine the kids at our school wanting to sign them.

'We need something quick and easy,' said Tanya. 'I remember Dad helped Ana with a petition to try and stop the closure of her daughter's school. Let's see if he still has it somewhere in his study. He hates throwing things away, so if we look hard enough we can probably find it. Hopefully he'll be home from work soon so he can show us himself.'

The study was upstairs opposite Tanya's bedroom, with a beautiful floor to ceiling window overlooking the front garden, a curved corner desk and loads of plants. I was struck by the feeling that I would love to work in a room like that in the future.

As I peered through the window, I imagined, for a second, what it would be like to swap lives with

Tanya – to have your own garden, a huge kitchen to cook in and loads of space. But the daydream was shattered when, behind me, Tanya screamed. I spun around.

She was staring at some papers on her dad's desk, a look of horror on her face.

'No way,' she said. 'No way. He can't have done.'

'What is it?'

'Look.'

I walked over to see what she was staring at and saw a big architectural sketch of a two-storey building. And then I spotted it – along the side were the words *Skipton House*. Tanya picked up the diagram, as if she wanted to rip it to shreds, and I held her arm to stop her. Under the diagram, was a folder of documents with the title, *Skipton House Sale*. I carefully peered inside. The first document had *Deed of Sale* written across the top. Below it was the name of the seller, and underneath that next to the word *Buyer* was Tanya's dad's name, *Robert Anukem*.

'Oh, Erin...' said Tanya, and her voice cracked as she started to cry. 'It's my dad. The buyer of Skipton House is my dad. How *could* he?'

'Hold on.' I desperately tried to collect my thoughts. 'It might not be what it seems—'

'It *is* what it seems. His name's on the documents! It couldn't be more obvious.' She covered her face with her hands and turned away from me. I went to give her a hug and it was then that we heard the front door slam.

'Hey. Anyone home?' called a man's voice from downstairs and Tanya's eyes widened with panic.

'Right, we can't say anything to him. We need to think this through,' I whispered to her. 'Let's go downstairs and stay calm.'

Tanya dabbed the tears from her cheeks. I squeezed her hand, but I felt a pang of anxiety about the idea of facing Tanya's dad. But as we walked into the kitchen there he was, exactly like the photo I'd seen – tall, smiling and relaxed. He smiled at us straight away, which made the whole situation much worse.

'Hi, you must be Erin?'

'Yeah. I'm Tanya's school friend.'

'I know. I've heard loads about you. We must have missed each other when you've come before. So what have you girls been up to?'

'Oh you know, not much. Homework,' said Tanya, in a tone that, unusually for her, sounded completely unconvincing.

I saw her dad raise an eyebrow, but he didn't say anything.

'Ana and Jayden should be back from swimming soon. Have you had dinner?'

'Not yet. I was waiting for Ana. She said that there was something for dinner that just needed some finishing touches.'

'Exactly – but did she tell you it's me who's cooking? I had a sudden urge to make beef nachos today. I even started them before I went out. See how prepared I am?' he said winking, and a shiver went down my spine. I couldn't believe this lovely man could have done something so awful.

Tanya sat at the kitchen table not saying anything and the situation was so awkward that I was desperate to go home, but I didn't want to leave Tanya. To make matters worse, her dad decided to bring up Cooking Club.

'Thanks for encouraging Tanya to go with you,' he said to me. 'It sounds like it's a great club and you've definitely learned some interesting dishes, haven't you?'

'Yeah, it's been good,' I agreed. 'My mum runs it now, and we erm… we're actually trying to find a new venue in which to hold it, because the old one's shutting down.'

I thought I saw an odd expression flit across his face as I spoke, but it was gone in an instant.

'Well, I have a good feeling that something will come up,' he said, smiling at me, as he put the finishing touches on the chilli beef. 'Come, join us for dinner. We've got plenty to eat.'

The food both smelled and tasted gorgeous, which surprised me. It was a shame that both Tanya and I had entirely lost our appetites.

Twenty-one

Tanya's mood hadn't improved in the slightest by Wednesday, and we held an urgent meeting at morning break to tell the boys about our terrible discovery.

'I honestly didn't know,' said Tanya, in a tiny voice. 'Please don't hate me.'

'It's nothing to do with you,' said Sam gently, although I could tell how shocked he was.

'Maybe he has no idea about how important it is to everyone,' said Frixos, perplexed. 'Is that possible?'

'I don't think so,' said Tanya. 'That's the most terrible part. When Jayden was younger he used to take him to football there. And he knows about Cooking Club – he'd been encouraging me to go for months, even before we met you, Erin. I don't understand why he would be so selfish. Sure, it's a good business opportunity, but what about all the people who use it and rely on it? Bad luck to them – and by them, I mean us. You should have seen how calm he was when he said that a new venue would probably crop up for Cooking Club. I don't get it.'

'There must be some explanation for it,' said Sam. 'Maybe there's something that we don't know.'

'I agree with Sam,' I said. 'But we should still treat him like we would any other Skipton buyer. You know, when you first mentioned doing a petition, I thought we should take it to Edgar, but maybe it doesn't matter that he never bothered to reply to us. Because now I think we should hand it to Tanya's dad. That way he'll see how much the place means to everyone. We don't need to print anything fancy. Let's keep it simple and gather the signatures.'

The boys secretly printed out a series of sheets in their IT lesson titled *Save Skipton* with a table below for names and signatures.

Then at lunchtime, we wolfed our sandwiches and got to work. Frixos found Gabriel in the sixth form common room and asked for his help in getting the petition round his year group. I took on our year, Tanya selected the Year Eights and Sam did the Year Nines. There was no way that we would be able to get round the whole school in a day, but this would be a good start.

I'd never done anything like it before, and at first I felt super awkward interrupting people, but I soon found that the vast majority of them were really friendly and loads signed their names. Some even wrote a little note next to their signature, saying what the community centre meant to them, such as, *Long Live Skipton Football Team founded at Skipton House!* or *Thank you Skipton House Dance Society for teaching me the coolest moves.* Lots of them didn't know about the planned closure and they were devastated to hear the news.

In form time that afternoon we tallied up our numbers. Tanya and I had almost a hundred signatures each.

'How many did you get?' I asked Frixos, who bumped into me on the way to English.

'I've got a hundred and thirty-three, but Sam did

better – he's got more than a hundred and fifty. He ended up getting started on the Year Tens too!'

'Incredible – that means we must have close to four hundred so far,' I said, doing some lightning mental maths.

'Let's meet at the gates after school to see if we can get more.'

I messaged Lara to say that I'd be late home because of the petition, and together with the boys we stood outside the gates, capturing anyone who hadn't yet signed and wanted to. This stage was even easier, as those who'd already given their signatures pointed us out to their friends, and people came up to us in groups.

'Right,' said Tanya triumphantly, when we reached six hundred names. 'I wonder what he'll say to this! I'd really like to hear him explain himself!'

'Don't hand it to him on your own,' said Sam, taking the petition out of her hands. 'You're angry – understandably – and you might say something that you regret. Plus, I think we'd all like to be there to help you. We're in this together, the Cooking Club Detectives – every one of us.'

'Yeah, absolutely,' Frixos and I said together.

'Let's wait until tomorrow night,' I suggested, 'and then we could all speak to him. Maybe you could tell him that you have something super important to say to him to make sure he'll be there?'

I thought Tanya was going to protest. I could see how tense she was, but her shoulders seemed to relax when she heard that we'd be there with her.

'You're right,' she said, 'that sounds like a better plan. And – I just wanted to say – thanks for helping and not turning your backs on me. It means a lot.'

'Hey, like Sam said, we're the Cooking Club Detectives,' I told her. 'This doesn't change anything.'

So we had a group hug and we finalised our plan of action for what would be the most important day in the campaign to save Skipton.

Twenty-two

Next day, as soon as the end of school bell went, we set off together to Tanya's house.

'I'm glad it's finally happening,' she told us. 'I haven't been able to face Dad the past couple of days and I can tell he's started to get worried about me. He was about to have a chat with me this morning, but I managed to get out of it by saying that I wanted to walk to school by myself. Anyway, at least we can speak to him properly for once. Ana said she'll help Jayden with his homework so we can talk downstairs.'

'Was she shocked?'

'Completely. But I could tell she didn't want to say anything bad about Dad.'

'We're here for you,' I said, squeezing her hand as she turned the key in the front door lock.

'Tanya, is that you?' Rob's voice called from the kitchen. The four of us piled in. He was making a cup of tea, but he stopped abruptly when he saw our whole gang.

'Oh, hello everyone,' he said, smiling. 'I didn't know you were all coming.'

'Dad, could you sit down for a second?' Tanya asked. Her voice was calm but we could hear the anger in it.

I could tell that her dad could hear it too. He sat down on one of the kitchen chairs. We did the same.

'Has something happened?' he asked.

'Yes, something *has* happened, and you know very well what it is.'

'I have no idea, Tanya. I'd rather you told me, because I'm beginning to get pretty worried. You haven't been yourself for a couple of days.'

'And neither have you, Dad!' Tanya said, handing him a neat black folder with all of our petition signatures.

Tanya's dad looked puzzled as he took it from her and opened it. And then the puzzlement on his face turned to wonder as he looked through the pages, taking the time to read the individual comments.

'There are so many. It's incredible. Did you collect these?' he asked. 'But why?'

'Why?' shouted Tanya, furious with his reaction. 'Because you're buying it. That's why.' Frixos caught her eye, and she tried to calm her voice. 'I went into your study the other day because I wanted to get your help with saving Skipton House. We've been worrying about it ever since we found out that it was going to be closed, and we've been working hard to hunt down whoever it is who is buying it, stupidly hoping that we might be able to change their mind. We've spent ages chasing potential leads, which got us nowhere. And do you know why? Because all of this time, the person who's buying Skipton is right here in my house and he didn't say anything,' said Tanya, pounding her fist on the table. Tears were rolling down her cheeks now.

'Tanya—'

'How could you? Do you know how many people love that place?'

'I've been going there since I was a child,' said

Sam, suddenly speaking up in a way that I'd never heard before. 'I went to day care there when I was little so my mum and my grandma could go to work. We used the food bank in the early days, while Mum got back on her feet. Later, I went to football club there, which was great fun, and most importantly it was free – otherwise I would have never been able to go. Frixos and I go to music club, it has the best breakfast ever, and we all go to Cooking Club. I think Tanya's told you about that.'

'She has.' His voice was tiny now, struggling to escape – like a cornered animal.

'So why do you want to take it away from us?' I asked him. I couldn't stop the outrage in my voice. 'And it's not just us. There are so many things that happen at that centre which the whole community benefits from.'

Rob breathed out slowly and put his face in his hands. When he looked up, I noticed that his gaze rested on Tanya.

'I'm very glad you brought me this,' he said, and his voice shook. It took him a while to calm down enough to carry on speaking. 'It reaffirms that I did the right thing. Tanya, you lost your mum really young, and I know that you and Jayden must miss her every day. I know I do. I wake up some days and hope that some wrinkle in time might have happened and that she'll still be here with us. But I promised her that I'd take care of you, because we both worked so hard to make sure that you had a lovely home, and everything you wanted. And that you're happy – there's nothing that matters to me more. It makes me sad to hear that you think I would have bought Skipton to make a profit out of it.'

'OK. But why…?'

'I want to tell you part of my story – a part that you haven't heard before. You don't know this, but when I was your age I lived in a tiny flat on an estate in North London. My two brothers, your uncles, shared a bedroom with me. Things were OK for a while, and we struggled through, but when your grandfather lost his job at the factory, we sometimes went hungry. So I know where you're coming from,' he said, looking at Sam.

'For a long while, life seemed pretty hopeless. It wasn't until one of my friends encouraged me to go to a community centre much like Skipton, that things started looking up. It ended up turning my world around.' He coughed to try and hide his emotion and brushed his hand across his eyes.

'So, when I saw the state that Skipton House was in, and how valuable it is to everyone here – it was a no-brainer. I have savings and I thought that there couldn't be a better cause to invest in. I want to improve it, do some major repairs to the building, and put in some proper tennis courts and football pitches, so that kids can feel proud of playing there. I didn't want the people who use it to be constantly worrying that things would break and that there wouldn't be any money to repair them. Or for them to be ashamed that the place they played and learned in looked so ramshackle.'

'So you're doing all these repairs?' asked Tanya quietly, not daring to believe it.

'I wanted to keep it a surprise, because I guessed how much it would mean to you and your friends. I was going to tell you on your birthday. Thinking about it now, that was a silly idea. You're a very intelligent girl and I should have known that you would start looking into what was going on with the centre. I suppose I didn't expect you to act so fast.'

Tanya's eyes were widening as he continued to talk and now we watched as she went over, wiping the tears from her face, and gave him a hug.

'I couldn't wait to tell you,' Rob continued. 'Every time I was stuck on the phone to the lawyers about some complicated issue, every time new problems cropped up in the redevelopment project, which gave me a headache, I thought about your reaction – all of you – when you heard the news.'

'I'm so sorry for what I said,' said Sam.

'And me too – sorry for accusing you,' I added, feeling hugely embarrassed.

'We shouldn't have assumed,' said Frixos. 'But our petition shows how grateful many people will be for what you're doing.'

'Thank you,' said Rob, hugging Tanya tight. 'I promise you that I'm going to do my very best to do a speedy renovation so that you can carry on with your clubs as you did before. I've actually got planning permission to build an extra floor. I'm hoping with more space we can provide further activities for even more kids.'

'And they'll still be free?'

'Yes, absolutely. That won't change.'

'You're the best,' said Sam, and I'd never seen him smile the way that he did then.

'You'll never guess what I've found out!' I shouted at Lara the minute I got back home.

'What?'

I'd already told her about what had happened the previous afternoon, and she'd offered to come with us to try to persuade Tanya's dad not to go through with the purchase. But I'd insisted that the Cooking Club Detectives could do this on their own. So she was eagerly awaiting the outcome of our quest.

'Skipton House can stay open! Rob was always intending to buy it and keep it as a community centre, only better – he's renovating the building and hopefully growing it! He's not planning to transform it into something else.'

'No way! And Tanya had no idea?' Lara was

so shocked that I noticed the mug of tea she was holding was slowly spilling onto the sofa.

'No. He was trying to keep it as a surprise for her until her birthday – because he knew how much it meant to all of us.'

'Oh Erin, that's the best news! Let me ring Molly. We need to celebrate.'

We ended up going to Sam's house with Lara's chicken pie and a bottle of lemonade. Molly was having a better day with her joint pain and had been in a fantastic mood ever since Sam had told her what had happened. Later, Sam's mum came home from work. She was lovely, with the same shy smile as his.

'Bless that wonderful man,' she said. 'He clearly has a good heart. He's not doing this for the money.'

'No, he said that he went to a similar place himself when he was our age. He understands how important it is to us,' said Sam. 'It looks like he's done really well since then too.'

'Good on him. It goes to show what having the right support means to people. I feel as though we need to have a proper party to celebrate this,' Molly decided.

'There's going to be a big one after the centre reopens,' I said. 'Tanya's dad said that he will try to minimise disruption to our clubs, but parts of the building will be closed for about two months, and they're going to start the work in early January. So we can help him plan something huge for March!'

'Excellent. It gives us time to learn how to make some more party dishes at Cooking Club in the meantime,' Lara smiled.

It was dark when we were walking home from Sam's, and Lara suddenly put her arm around me.

'I was thinking about how proud you make me,' she said. 'You went to such efforts to save the community centre. I know that in the end it turned out that we didn't have to worry, but it shows that in the future, you'll be ready to fight for the things you know matter.'

'Well, it's you who taught me that,' I said honestly and it felt like the right moment to tell her everything I'd been bottling up for the past few months. 'I've been feeling quite guilty actually.'

'Guilty? Why? What have you done now?' asked Lara, winking.

'Nothing. It's more about what I've stopped *you* from doing. I thought that having me meant that you couldn't pursue your dream of being a famous chef. When you decided that you wanted to give cooking a proper go as a career after you got made redundant, I realised how much you wanted it and I felt guilty for getting in the way.'

Lara stopped walking. We were almost outside our flat and the lights from our neighbours' windows illuminated her face. She looked shocked and sad.

'Oh, Erin. I wish you'd said. I would have told you straight away that there is nothing – not cooking, not running a blog, not having a successful business, or loads of money – that is more important to me than you. Besides, that other stuff would be absolutely meaningless if I didn't have you. Who would I celebrate my successes with? Who would enjoy the food that we cook together? Maybe I don't tell you this enough, and I'm sorry if that's the case. I think I've been so wrapped up in this whirlwind of the blog and Cooking Club, that we haven't spoken enough about the important things.'

'I think deep down I knew I shouldn't feel

guilty,' I admitted, hugging her tightly. 'And, also – I read your diary entries in the recipe book from when you were pregnant.'

'You did? I haven't read them in years, you know. But I remember that I was so excited to meet you, especially when it got close to you being born! Shall we go and have a look now?'

So we both wiped our eyes, and went upstairs. And then we read two diary entries together, which would stay with me for ages, and make me realise exactly how she felt about me.

 2nd October 2009

The summer extended well into September this year, but it's over now and I've moved in with Mum. At first it felt like going back in time because I haven't lived here for so long. But it's nice to be here. The big news is that I was right. The scan revealed that I'm having a girl! I've decided to call her Erin, after several strong ladies from Mum's family.

We even had some banana bread today to celebrate the scan going well and it reminded me of Rob. I wonder what he's up to these days.

24th December 2009

It's been the most wonderful Christmas Eve. We went to Sarah's for mince pies, and Mum and I are now at home adding the finishing touches to Erin's little cot bed — given as a present to us by Rodrigo. What a lovely surprise that was! Mum's finished knitting Erin's blanket and we've added some animal pictures to her side of the room to brighten it up.

I have a feeling that she'll be an inquisitive young lady! As of last week, I've officially stopped work for six months which means that I'll have loads of time to look after her and get to know her. I've never been so thrilled! I have a feeling that we will be best friends.

But before I leave this book for a while to focus on much more important things, I must remember to add the recipe for a lovely cottage pie, which Mum and I (and Erin!) have really been enjoying in the run-up to Christmas. I can't wait for a time when Erin and I will be able to cook together!

Twenty-three

After we'd solved the mystery of the Skipton buyer, the rest of term seemed to speed by. Lara and I made her cottage pie several times in December, and then focused on perfecting some new Christmas recipes for her blog, which included orange-flavoured mince pies and the most delicious bacon roast potatoes. Tanya and her family went skiing for the winter break, but as soon as they were back in January, the Cooking Club Detectives gathered at her house to plan Skipton's reopening party.

'It would be nice to give it some structure,' said Rob, as we sat down once again around the table where he'd first told us his news. 'I was thinking that we could ask some of the different clubs if they'd like to contribute. Perhaps the dance group could put on a show? And would you guys at Cooking Club be able to help us out with the food?'

'Definitely. I'll speak to my mum,' I said. 'Wouldn't it also be great if we did something live on the day though? I was thinking about a baking competition. What does everyone think?'

'Hey, that's a good idea. Could I leave it to you to organise that? I still have lots of work to do overseeing the renovations so I'd be grateful for any help you can give me.'

'No problem. Leave it to us!' I said. I think we still felt guilty about the way we'd accused Tanya's dad and we wanted to do the best we could to make it up to him.

So Tanya and Frixos spoke to Mr Chandler and got the club leaders involved in arranging their contributions to the party, and I got to work with Lara on planning both the menu and the baking competition. We couldn't do it by ourselves, so Lara contacted a catering team who had once reached out to her via the blog, and planned a series of recipes that would provide something for everyone.

'I've had a wild idea,' said Lara. 'This is a proper

233

celebration, isn't it? And I'm judging the baking competition?'

'Both of these things are true,' I agreed.

'So what I think I'll do is… get everyone to make banana bread!'

'Finally!' I said. 'I'm so glad you chose that!'

'Well, we haven't had a proper, *proper* celebration until now and…'

'… Banana bread is only for *proper* celebrations. You'd better organise loads of bananas then! And I think you should make it a blind test – so that it's fair. Otherwise, you might choose me because I'm your favourite.'

'Perfect,' she agreed. 'And that means you have a chance of winning through your own baking ability and not because I'm biased.'

The party took place on a wonderful sunny Saturday in April, right after the Easter holidays. More than three hundred people had confirmed that they were coming on the online guestlist.

'I've never been so nervous in my life,' said Lara as she paced the kitchen the night before. 'What if they hate it?'

'Hate what? The food? You can stop worrying about that right now,' I told her, 'because you know that's impossible. It's totally delicious. Every one of your recipes is.'

'I don't think I'll sleep tonight. Also, there's something I've been meaning to tell you – we actually have another thing to celebrate. But I'm keeping it a secret until after the party.'

'You can't do that!' I said, suddenly feeling like Sausage who had been denied a treat. 'You can't tell me there's some exciting news and then keep me in suspense.'

'Of course, I can,' said Lara. 'I'm helping you practise being patient. It's a really key skill.'

Tanya, Frixos, Sam and I met early on Saturday to help set everything up. Tanya had a well-organised and tight schedule for the events and performances that would take place. They included a dance show, a keepy-uppy competition from the football club and a mini concert, as well as the banana bread judging.

'Dad's also giving a speech,' she told us as we were laying out the cutlery.

The party was due to start at three p.m, and an hour earlier, we went home to get changed. Lara was wearing her bright blue dress. I was feeling summery, so I put on my lemon-yellow jeans and a shimmery green top that Lara had made for me. Sausage was wearing a bright red bow tie that we'd found at the bottom of my toy chest which kept coming undone as he leaped around with excitement.

I was amazed at how many people turned up. Most of our year group at school was there, and I recognised kids from other years too. Then there were some important-looking people in suits – I guessed that they might be from the local council – as well as the entire football team, who were helping to hand out drinks before Rob's speech.

He made his way to the steps leading to the door of Skipton House. We gathered around him in the front garden.

'Hello, everyone, and welcome to the grand opening of Skipton House community centre. I'm so happy to be here, and pleased that our building work is complete. In a short while, you'll be able to admire a place that you know and love, but which is bigger, safer, and can last us for many more years to come.'

There was a big round of applause and people clinking glasses.

'I know that many of you have benefitted from coming to Skipton over the years, and I wanted to thank my daughter, Tanya, and her friends, Erin, Sam and Frixos, for reminding me exactly how much this centre means to everyone. You'll be pleased to hear that the cooking club, music breakfasts, yoga, dance and pretty much all of your other sessions can now resume, and you'll be able to view the new timetable on our website and also on the notice boards outside reception.

'And now, we have a series of fabulous performances to watch from various clubs and societies. Please enjoy the wonderful food and have an absolutely great time!'

I was clapping so hard that I almost missed the expression on Lara's face. She was concentrating hard on the speech and looking at Rob with a mixture of amazement and confusion.

We watched all the performances, which were incredible. I didn't have a clue about some of the things that the other groups got up to, and I made a mental note to ask if I could join the dance club. That is if they would agree to take a tall and gangly total beginner. Then Lara took over the microphone and announced the start of the cooking competition.

'Thank you to everyone who has been coming to Cooking Club,' she said. 'I know we're keen to get back to creating some delicious dishes at the brand new community centre. But first, I thought that we could kick things off by making everyone here an extra special dessert and in doing so, we could have a little competition to see which pair of bakers does it best. I've set up our work benches for the mixing of ingredients, and our wonderful catering team will help with putting everything in the oven when it's ready. Today we are making banana bread. I don't know about you, Rob, but for

me, it has always been associated with celebration.'
I could see her cast a strange look in Tanya's dad's direction.

And then I stopped stirring as I watched the two of them walk towards each other laughing. They gave each other an enormous hug.

'I can't believe it's you!' I heard Lara say.

'Hey, does your dad know my mum?' I asked Tanya, nudging her. 'Look over there.'

'I don't think so. Where would they have met and when?'

'It seems as if they've known each other for ages. They look like they've been friends for years.'

'They're so happy. Are we missing something?'

Needless to say, Tanya and I didn't win the competition. A couple of Year Eight boys did. Our banana bread was lumpy, with not enough sugar. In fact, it was possibly our worst effort ever. But we had a very good reason. We were engrossed in watching our parents, who looked absolutely delighted to see each other. I can't remember Lara ever being so delighted. We went over to them as soon as we possibly could.

'Girls, you would never believe it!' said Lara. 'This is Rob. My friend from when I was your age!'

'Do you remember when you came to me that day with the petition and I told you about the friend who encouraged me to go to my community centre all those years ago?' asked Tanya's dad. 'Well, this is her! She got me to sign up for the football club, and I later became team captain and everything changed for me.'

'No way!'

'The very same person.'

They spent the rest of the party sitting together on a bench trying to catch up on everything that had happened during the years they'd been out of touch. They had mutual friends that they remembered, and they asked about each other's families. The weirdest part, of course, was that Rob already knew me, and Tanya already knew Lara. In some ways it seemed as though the two of them had never been apart.

'I knew you'd always repay the favour when I got you into that club,' said Lara to Rob when we started dancing. Soon Ana, Jayden, Frixos and Sam joined in, and then Sam's mum and grandma came over too. Molly managed a good ten minutes on the dance floor before she had to have a rest. Lara looked amazing. I'd never enjoyed myself so much, and for the first time I didn't worry about looking awkward.

Loads of people came to thank Rob for keeping the community centre not only open, but much improved and Mr Chandler was particularly impressed when he heard our story of everyone we'd managed to investigate.

'Come for dinner tomorrow. You're both welcome whenever you want,' Rob said to us. 'I mean it!'

'We'll take you up on that!' Lara promised, laughing.

By the time we'd finished clearing up, it was almost eleven p.m, and when we got home, Lara and I were shattered.

'I won't let you go to sleep before you reveal what the other surprise is,' I told her as we collapsed onto her double bed. 'I haven't forgotten.'

'Well remembered! So… I've been approached by quite a big cooking school in London. They've asked if I could be one of their chefs, running classes twice, maybe three times a week. It's good hours – when you're at school – and pretty easy to get to on the train. I'll still be able to do Cooking Club too and on the days that I'm not working, I can keep my blog up to date. And last, but not least, it's good money.'

'That's fantastic, Mum!'

'Isn't it? It's thanks to you. Truly. Because without you, I never would have properly started the blog, and I certainly wouldn't have found out how much I loved running the club. It made me realise I wasn't made for sitting at home alone. Promoting yourself online and having a huge following is great, especially if it gets the word out there to people who think that cooking healthy meals means spending loads of money on ingredients – but I love being around others, and I particularly love teaching.'

'You're welcome,' I said, and together with Sausage, we had a three-way hug.

Erin's Banana Bread Bonanza

Ingredients

- 2 very ripe bananas
- 150g butter
- 150g caster sugar
- 2 large eggs
- 150g self-raising flour
- 50g icing sugar
- 1 small tub of vanilla ice cream

Method

1. Heat the oven to 180°C. Grease a loaf tin (around 25 x 15 cm) with butter.

2. Mash bananas with a fork in a bowl.

3. Get a medium-sized bowl and add the butter and caster sugar. Mix together by hand using a spoon, or with an electric hand mixer if you have one.

4. Then crack two eggs into a separate bowl and whisk. Add the whisked eggs

to the butter and sugar and stir. Then fold in the mashed bananas and flour.

5. When soft and creamy, add the mixture to the tin and put in the oven for 30 minutes. Check whether the loaf is cooked through by piercing the centre with a skewer.

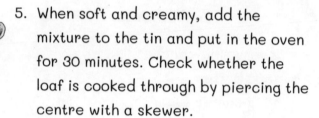

6. When the loaf is cool, dust with icing sugar and serve with generous dollops of vanilla ice cream.

7. Celebrate!

A letter to you from Ewa

Hello there,

Are you a devourer of mysteries, like me? I love turning the pages and trying to figure out the clues, just like a real detective. I have to admit that I don't always get it right. I hope you enjoyed Erin, Tanya, Frixos and Sam's detective work. Did you guess who the culprit was?

I thought I could tell you a little about how I came up with *The Cooking Club Detectives*. When I volunteered at a school in London, we had breakfast provided every morning by a charity called Magic Breakfast. It was open to everyone, but many of the children who used it had not had any food that day at home. We all know that food is important fuel for learning, but having breakfasts together also started new friendships.

In writing my story, I wanted to show what an important role community plays in our lives. Erin, Tanya, Frixos and Sam attend the cooking club held at their local community centre, which also provides a breakfast club, free sports lessons and daycare for younger children. The four friends know that there will always be someone supportive there who can offer a helping hand if they need it. We may all go through times when we are struggling with something, and some of us might think we need to try to carry on without telling anyone. But this is what our families, friends and teachers are there for – to offer support

If you're going through a hard time for whatever reason, please share your experience with someone you trust. I'm sure that like Sam, you'll find that it makes all the difference.

Ewa

magic
breakfast
fuel for learning

If you are hungry, it's hard concentrate in class. Magic Breakfast provides healthy breakfasts in lots of schools in the UK to make sure everyone can make the most of their morning lessons, particularly those who haven't had much to eat at home.

To learn more about what Magic Breakfast does, and for ideas on how you can help fundraise or campaign for this wonderful charity, check out their website:

www.magicbreakfast.com

Magic Breakfast's website also has a special section on nutrition, where you can find healthy, nutritious recipes to add to the ones in this book and information on how the food we eat helps power and protect our bodies.

Acknowledgements

There are many people who contributed to bringing this book to life.

Thank you to my agent Kate Hordern, for all her great advice on early drafts and general agent-y wisdom.

Thank you to the amazing team at Zephyr - Fiona, Lauren, Jade and Meg for their invaluable input and the attention that they paid to helping me get this story as good as it can be. It started out life as a very different book!

I would also like to thank my fabulous illustrator Katy Riddell, who so wonderfully brought Erin, Tanya, Frixos and Sam to life.

A big thank you to all the staff at Magic Breakfast, who provide healthy breakfasts to children who might otherwise go hungry. You inspired *The Cooking Club Detectives*, and I hope that I can in a small way contribute to your amazing work.

Thank you to Alex Cunningham for the insightful interview and for taking the time to tell me how the charity was founded and why it's so very needed in schools around the UK. A big thank you also to Jo Matthews and Katy Ellis for all your enthusiasm and encouragement.

Thank you to my family and friends for your ongoing support - for being a sounding board for plot ideas and for helping me come up with character names.

And finally, a big thanks to you, dear readers. You're the people that make the magic happen. Thank you for choosing my book. I hope you enjoyed it!

Ewa Jozefkowicz
London
March 2021